Commission on Boston Harbor

Special Report of the United States Commissioners on

Boston Harbor

on the relation of Mystic Pond and River to Boston Harbor, 1861 - Vol. 1

Commission on Boston Harbor

Special Report of the United States Commissioners on Boston Harbor
on the relation of Mystic Pond and River to Boston Harbor, 1861 - Vol. 1

ISBN/EAN: 9783337382438

Printed in Europe, USA, Canada, Australia, Japan

Cover: Foto ©Andreas Hilbeck / pixelio.de

More available books at **www.hansebooks.com**

SPECIAL REPORT

OF THE UNITED STATES

COMMISSIONERS ON BOSTON HARBOR,

ON THE RELATION OF

MYSTIC POND AND RIVER

TO

BOSTON HARBOR.

1861.

BOSTON:

GEO. C. RAND & AVERY, CITY PRINTERS,

No. 3 CORNHILL.

1861.

REPORT.

WASHINGTON, D. C., *Jan.* 15, 1861.

SIR : I have the honor to transmit to you the Report of the United States Harbor Commissioners, upon the subject of the proposed changes in Mystic Ponds and River (referred to in the communication of your predecessor, of January 24, 1860), which has been unavoidably delayed.

Very respectfully your obedient servant,

Jos. G. TOTTEN, Bt. Brig. Gen.,

U. S. Engineers.

His Honor J. M. WIGHTMAN,

Mayor of Boston.

WASHINGTON, D. C., *Dec.* 18, 1860.

GENTLEMEN : At the time when we had the honor to receive your communication of January 24, of this year, transmitting an order of the City Government, in which the opinion of the Commissioners upon the probable effect on the harbor, of certain proposed changes in the Mystic Pond and River was asked for, we had under review our plan of operations for the survey of Boston Harbor.

This plan embraced, among other things, a physical investigation into the motion of the waters of Boston Harbor and its tributaries.

We were about to submit to you our preliminary report, in which we had provided for a renewal, upon a more minute scale, of those tidal and current observations which had formerly been made by the Coast Survey of the United States, principally for hydrographical purposes.

Anticipating your concurrence in our proposed plan of proceeding, we thought it most judicious, and we may even say, most respectful, to defer an explicit reply to the inquiry, until our examinations were completed.

These examinations have since been made ; the materials of a more minute and comprehensive report have been collected, and time has been allowed us for giving to the question more study and reflection.

The subject is one of importance, and is entitled to mature consideration on many accounts, — not the least of which is, that our opinions may exercise an influence upon the future legislation concerning Boston Harbor, a matter of general interest to the nation.

We shall arrange what we have to say in reply to your inquiry, under the following heads : —

1. The examination of the Mystic Ponds, and of the River to its mouth.

2. The results of this examination in their relation to the Estuary alone.

3. The relation of the River and the Estuary, together with their affluents, to Boston Harbor.

4 . General remarks.

EXAMINATION OF THE MYSTIC PONDS, AND OF THE RIVER
TO ITS MOUTH.

The examination of the Mystic Ponds and River was
intended to be incidental to the more extensive physical inquiries instituted in the Harbor; and the instruc-
tions given to Assistant Mitchell, regarding this project,
directed *occasional* observations by detachments of his
party, and the compilation of some general notes, which
should enable us to judge of the value of Mystic River
in the regimen of the channels of Boston Harbor.

About the time that this work was to commence, the
Mayor of the city of Charlestown, Hon. James Dana,
directed C. L. Stevenson, Esq., a civil engineer of that
city, to renew and extend some of the examinations
undertaken a year since, regarding the propriety of
using the waters of the Mystic Ponds for supplying
the city. As the observations to be made by Mr.
Stevenson were to be, in many respects, similar to those
contemplated by Mr. Mitchell, an arrangement was
entered into between these gentlemen, by which they
united their parties, and thus were enabled to extend
their inquiries into many valuable details, which might
otherwise have been neglected for the want of time
and means.

We shall now proceed to describe, briefly, the nature
of the observations recorded, and the general conclusions to which they lead us.

Seven principal points were chosen, at which systematic observations of tides and currents were made
in series of from twelve to twenty-four hours in duration, and many of these points were occupied simulta-

neously, and the observations were frequently repeated. It was not deemed necessary to continue the observations very long at any single station, since they could if desirable, be referred to the Coast Survey tidal series at the Charlestown Dry Dock (which has been kept up for many years), and be thus reduced, in a general way to their mean conditions.

The stations referred to are "Upper Mystic Pond," "Lower Mystic Pond," "Weir Bridge," (outlet of Lower Pond,) "Wood's Mill," "Herring Weir," "Medford Bridge," and "Ten Hills." (See Sketch marked A.) To these, in the discussion of the results, we have added several stations near the mouth of the river, occupied more especially for the harbor work. The approximate distances of these stations from Charlestown Dry Dock, measured along the channel, are given in Table No. 1; and in the same table, the depths and areas of sections will also be found.

Diagrams A_1 and A_2 give the observations of tides at the points we have referred to; and B_1 the currents at the same and other points. These observations are represented in curves; the figures along the top of the diagrams indicating the hours of observation; those on the side, the heights of the tide, or the velocities of the currents. The tides are plotted above a common datum line, or zero, which is 5.50 feet below the mean low water of Boston Harbor; the flood and ebb velocities of the currents are plotted above and below a zero line which marks slack water. In these Diagrams, the observations are separated according to their dates; and where several series of results are obtained at the same station, it may be seen how variable the conditions are.

Diagrams A_3 and B_2 are attempted generalizations of the phenomena, intended to present comparative views of the results at different stations, freed from anomalous changes. The numerical results, which these two diagrams illustrate, may be found with other data, in Tables Nos. 2, 3, and 4.

Tides.—When we speak of the *tides,* we mean the vertical rise and fall of the water; when of the *currents,* its horizontal motion ; when of the *tidal currents,* the horizontal motion caused by the changes of level of the tides.

In reference to tidal action, the Mystic River may be divided into two parts; the one, from the harbor to some point between the Ten Hills Station and Medford Bridge, and near the latter, where the time and height of the tides are nearly the same as at the river mouth; and the other, from this point to the pond at which the duration of flood and ebb is abnormal, if considered with reference to tidal currents, and where the simple river regimen of downward currents predominates.

The curve aa' (see Diagram A_3) represents the tides as observed at Charlestown Dry Dock. It is normal in character, and has yet undergone but little change of form since leaving the ocean. From other observations made by the Coast Survey, it has been determined that the wave travels the entire distance from Boston Lower Light to the Charlestown Dry Dock in twelve minutes, and that all parts of the wave suffer the same delay in this journey. The changes of depth, from hour to hour, in the channels of the harbor, due to rise and fall of the tide, are not in so great ratio to the total depths of water, as materially to vary the friction, and thus to cause sensible irregularities in the rate of wave propagation.

Beyond the Dry Dock, as our point of observation advances up the Mystic River, we find the shallowe channels causing greater delays in the progress of th tide wave, and so varying their sections at differen stages of the tide, as to make this delay irregular, — being least at high water, and greatest at low wate The currents also vary the apparent rates of the wav motion, as we shall show.

The tide wave at Ten Hills, bb', is very slightly displaced to the right, upon our diagram, — it has suffered a delay of five minutes for high water and twenty-four for low water. The form of the curve cc', representing the tide at Medford Bridge, is sensibly disturbed from its position at the Navy Yard, — having suffered fourteen minutes delay in high water, and fifty-two minutes in low water. The tide wave is propagated with some regularity thus far, and for a certain distance beyond, though not so far as Herring Weir, where the curve dd' represents the law of rise and fall, and is sharply interrupted three hours before, and three and a half hours after, high water, suddenly changing to a nearly straight line on both flood and ebb when the level of 11.64 feet is reached. There are then sixteen inches of water in the thread of the stream, the bed of which is here about $4\frac{1}{4}$ feet above mean low water of the harbor. The curve ee' represents the corresponding phenomena at the dam at Wood's Mill. The form of the flood-tide curve is here but little, though somewhat affected after the rise commences; but that of the ebb is not a true tidal fall, even while the depth remains considerable. The

water must rise to about 12.8 feet above our datum line
before the tide commences its rise; and on the ebb, it
ceases to fall about the time that this plane is again
reached. High water occurs forty-two minutes later at
this place than at the Dry Dock, but the level reached
is about the same. The tide of Weir Bridge is shown
by the curve ff'. The horizontal of 14.15 feet represents the river ebb, and the depth of water is then $3\frac{1}{2}$
feet. The height reached by the tide is less than at
Wood's Mill, but high water occurs at nearly the same
time. The exceedingly small rise and fall in the upper
and lower Mystic Ponds, is represented by the curve
gg'. The tide-water is not admitted to the ponds in
sufficient quantity to vary their levels greatly. The
greatest rise and fall due to tides, given in Diagrams A_1
and A_2, is about $\frac{2}{10}$ feet, an inconsiderable quantity
when compared with the rise following the freshet of
September 13, as exhibited on Diagram A_2.

The surface of this pond, as shown on Diagram A_3
lies below high water of the Harbor; but it must be
remembered that these observations were made at a
dry season. We may state, generally, then, that *the tide
rises to the same absolute height, at high water, in all parts of
the Mystic River, from the Harbor to Wood's Mill, although
the delay in reaching its greatest altitude varies (increasingly)
as we ascend the river. It is only during the dry season that
Mystic Pond can be in any sense classed as a tidal reservoir,
and, even at this period, the presence of the tide in this basin
is to be discovered only by careful observation.*

Thus far, we have spoken of the tide as a wave. It
is propagated from sea at rates varying from fifty miles
an hour (its velocity from the entrance of the Harbor

2

to the Dry Dock) to about two miles an hour in the
upper portion of Mystic River. So rapid is the increase
of the permanent causes of delay (friction and the like)
in the latter portion of this journey, that the rate of
wave propagation becomes less than the possible velocity of running water; we are not to expect, therefore,
that the advance of the tide wave will be uniform, if
currents, even while the depth and section remain constant, traverse its path. At Wood's Mill, as we have
seen, the part of the tide above a certain height main-
tains its wave character as its rising portion advances
in a favoring, or only feebly opposing, stream; while
its falling portion, struggling onward against the combined opposition of river and ebb tidal current, is
retarded in such unequal ratios that the symmetry of
the figure is destroyed.

From what we shall have to say hereafter of the
currents, it will be understood that a very small increase of head in the Mystic Pond, without enlarging
the section very considerably at Wood's Mill, may make
the velocity greater than the rate of travel which we
have shown for the tide; at such times there may be
a gradual backing up of the stream, as by a dam, but
nothing like a symmetrical tide. The Herring Weir
tide shows also the peculiarities we have described as
presented at Wood's Mill. *Under ordinary circumstances,
Wood's Mill may be regarded as the point where the true tide
wave ceases.*

Currents. — Referring to Diagram B_2 and the tables
we have already mentioned, we find that at the station
off the Dry Dock the maximum of flood is reached at

about two to three hours after the slack water of ebb,
descending more gradually to the slack water of flood,
in about three or four hours, making the duration of
flood about five and a half hours; the mean from the
observations is 5h. 27m. The ebb exceeds in velocity
and duration the flood, owing to the river influence.
At Medford Bridge (curve ii'), the flood current rises
to a maximum of 1.50 miles per hour, in two and
three quarters hours from slack water, and declines in
two hours to the next slack, its duration being but
about 4h. 56m. The great excess of the ebb, as well as
the form of the flood-current curve, shows the influence
of the river waters, the depth and section. The duration of the prolonged ebb here is nearly seven and a
half hours.

At Wood's Mill (curve ll', the station lies below the
dam), the flood is small in velocity and duration, the
force of the flood tide from the harbor being exhausted
in checking the river current to about 1.35 miles per
hour, which runs steadily for ten and a half hours out
of twelve and a quarter.

At Weir Bridge (curve mm', Diagram B_2), the features are similar to those at Wood's Mill, the velocity
of the flood being increased at a maximum to 1.40
miles, and its duration diminished to one and three
quarters hours. The rapid increase of ebb velocity to
the point where the river current alone acts, uninflu-
enced by the tidal current, is well marked in the curves
for both Weir Bridge and Wood's Mill, by the horizontal
line denoting a constant current.

Let us now trace the hourly conditions of the river
during an entire tide. Diagrams C_1 and C_2, are made

out from tables already spoken of, and as many stations are used as the scale of the plotting will admit. C_1 corresponds to the flood, and C_2 to the ebb. The relative levels of the surface of the river are given for every hour as marked, and the direction and magnitude of the current at that time are shown by an arrow,— the direction by the head, and the velocity by the length of the shaft. Connecting the points of the arrows (by a broken line in sketch), we have the curves representing the velocities of flood and ebb. The time of slack water is shown as that in which these curves cross the axis. A section of the bottom of the river, and position of the pond, is given on the same diagram. The arrows of different stations are connected by a dotted line, to show the inclination of the water surface. From these diagrams we easily deduce the character of the river, as to tides and currents, at any time, corresponding to these observations.

When it is low water at Charlestown Dry Dock, the Mystic presents the following peculiarities: The surface is lower in the harbor than at Ten Hills Station, where it is not yet low water, and where there is little current. At Medford Bridge, the surface is 0.98 feet above the level of the water at Ten Hills, and there is a downward current of 1.68 miles per hour. At Herring Weir, the surface is 4.61 feet above the water-level at Medford Bridge, and a downward current of 1.36 miles prevails. At Wood's Mill, at this time, the surface is 1.19 feet higher than at Herring Weir, and there is a strong downward current of 1.36 miles per hour,— the Mystic Pond is pouring out its waters.

The tide rising, in about an hour the level of the

water at the Ten Hills Station is below that of the harbor and of Medford Bridge. A flood current prevails off the Dry Dock of 0.3 miles; while at Medford Bridge it is still flowing downward at the rate of 1.54 miles per hour. These two currents conflict in the space between these stations, and slack water occurs near Ten Hills. It is evident that whatever is brought in by the flood from the harbor, or down by the river, must be deposited at this time along the slack-water region. This slack current travelling up the river, as the point of greatest depression, does not reach Medford Bridge until above an hour after low water at the Dry Dock. The flood current reaches its maximum of 0.4 miles per hour at Ten Hills Station about two and a half hours after low water, declining slowly to the high-water stand, about eight minutes before high water. The current at the Ten Hills Station is a normal one, following the general law of the harbor currents.

At Medford Bridge, the flood current reaches a maximum of 1.31 miles at three hours from low water.

The level of Wood's Mill Station is reached by the waters at Ten Hills Station four and a quarter hours after low water, and by the water at Medford Bridge but a quarter of an hour later. Although the river is never actually level from its mouth to Wood's Mill, yet there is an approach to this condition four and a quarter hours after low water off the Dry Dock. At this time there is a flood current of 0.30 miles off Dry Dock, and at Ten Hills; of 1.17 miles at Medford Bridge, and a downward current of 1.20 at Wood's Mill.

About one hour before slack current of flood at Ten
Hills, the river has reached the level of the Mystic
Pond, and after this time flows into it. About the time
of slack current at Ten Hills, the flood current at
Wood's Mill has a velocity of 0.44 miles. The duration of flood current at Ten Hills is nearly 5h. 50m.;
at Medford Bridge, 4h. 56m.; at Wood's Mill, about 1h.
46m.; and about the same at the entrance to the
pond.

The ebb current at Ten Hills increases to a maximum
of 0.60 miles per hour, three and a half hours after
high water, and continues at a nearly uniform velocity
for two hours; after which it declines rapidly, reaching
its slack after a duration of 6h. 45m. The ebb current
begins at Wood's Mill about three quarters of an hour
after local high water, increasing in two hours to a
velocity of 1.30, and in three and a half hours to a
velocity of 1.40 miles, from which it varies ·but little
through seven and a half hours. At this point the ebb
current (downward) runs ten and a half hours.

At Medford Bridge, the ebb current begins only
twenty minutes after local high water. It lasts about
seven and a half hours.

On Diagrams D_1 and D_2 are given comparative views
of the durations of the flood currents, and the durations
of slack water from station to station. In the first of
the diagrams, the influence of land waters can be
traced, these having a tendency to destroy the flood
current, or shorten its duration. The duration of this
current increases as we leave the Mystic Pond, and
descend the river, reaching a maximum at Ten Hills,
and diminishing but little at a station near the Boston

and Maine Railroad Bridge. Below this the Malden
River debouches; and at the station between Chelsea
and Malden bridges, — notwithstanding the Mystic has
here a great section, — the duration of flood lessens
to the same value as at Medford Bridge. In the deep
waters off Charlestown Navy Yard, the duration of
flood again increases, but by reason of the influx of
several more land streams, the flood, even here, does not
regain the duration observed at Ten Hills. The capacity of the channel at Ten Hills is to that at the Navy
Yard as 1 to 40 for low water, and as 1 to 10 for high
water; so that the little influence which the Mystic
Pond, Alewive Brook, and other feeders of the river
have, as low down as Ten Hills, can scarcely affect the
times of the current at Charlestown Navy Yard, especially at low water. We are safe in asserting, therefore, that *the outflow of Mystic Pond does not produce a
measurable effect upon the times of the currents in Boston
Harbor below Charlestown.*

The upper portion of the Mystic River is traversed
by a predominating ebb stream of considerable scouring power, which no doubt wears away its gravelly
bed gradually, and deposits the debris at a lower point
in the river, perhaps below Ten Hills, where the feeble
currents are interrupted by long periods of slack
water, which offer opportunities for deposits. On Diagram D_2, the comparative durations of slack water
are exhibited. The greatest duration occurs between
flood and ebb, at the Boston and Maine Railroad
Bridge.

If we assume that one half the difference between
the maximum velocities of ebb and flood is the velocity

of the outflow of land waters, (this supposition is not exact, but is not greatly in error,) this would give, for the velocity of the outflow at Ten Hills, about one tenth of a mile per hour at the season of our observations, — *a force which would be inadequate of itself to effect any scour; but, united with tidal currents, it has become an important element in the maintenance of the channel of the estuary.*

Results of this Examination in their Relation to the Estuary alone.

De La Beche, in his memorandum on estuaries and their tides, has justly observed that the present and actual state of any estuary, or tidal river, may be considered as an *adjustment*, for the time, of the several parts or materials of which it is formed. So also the *regimen* of a river is correctly defined to be a state in which the bed of the stream is equal to the reception and discharge of all the waters (whether river or tidal) that it can be required to pass; and further, the resultant of all the conflicting forces that act upon it, by means of which regularity and uniformity of motion in the stream are preserved, and the same flow is secured under similar circumstances.

We have just seen what the adjustment and regimen of the Mystic River and Estuary are at the present time. We have seen —

1. *That it is only during the dry season that Mystic Pond can be classed as a tidal reservoir; and that even then the presence of the tide wave in the basin is scarcely appreciable.*

2. *That under ordinary circumstances Wood's Mill may be regarded as the point at which the true tide ceases.*

3. *That at Wood's Mill the ebb (downward) current runs ten and a half hours, and that at Medford Bridge, it lasts about seven and a half hours.*

4. *That the influence of land waters tends to destroy the flood current, or shorten its duration; that this duration reaches its maximum in descending the river at Ten Hills ; and further, below the Railroad Bridge, where Malden River falls into the Mystic, notwithstanding the increased section of the latter, the duration of the flood is again diminished to the same period as at Medford Bridge.*

5. *That even in the deep waters off Charlestown Navy Yard, by reason of the influx of several more land streams, the flood does not regain the same period of duration that it had at Ten Hills.*

6. It will be observed, we are speaking here of the effect of the influx of the lower streams upon the duration of the tide, and not of Mystic Pond, Alewive Brook, and other upper feeders of the river.

7. In relation to the latter we have observed that *the outflow of Mystic Pond does not produce a measurable effect upon the times of the currents in Boston Harbor below Charlestown.*

8. *And finally, that the velocity of the outflow, being added to that of the tidal current, forms an important element in the maintainance of the estuary of the channel.*

This last deduction is the consummate result and consequence of all the preceding conclusions ; and points out the nature of the relation existing between the estuary of the Mystic, and the tide and river waters above that estuary.

That relation may be embodied, in general terms, in the following statement : —

3

If the materials forming the bed of a stream are of the rolling description, as sand and gravel, land streams, having velocities less than one-half mile per hour are quite inadequate to their removal. Again, if a channel is traversed by equal and opposite tidal streams, however violent, the rolling material forming its bed is but borne to and fro without ultimate removal. But, if the channel of a river is traversed by both land streams and tidal currents, with conditions as above, a very considerable scouring power may be the result, and the material may be permanently removed. If a flood current fails to set in motion a pebble which it encounters, it is because the force is exhausted in overcoming the inertia and friction; but this force, if aided by the ebb-tidal current, may become powerful enough to roll this pebble a considerable distance; while, on the other hand, the same force, by resisting the flood-tidal current, prevents the return of the pebble; and thus it makes a daily seaward gain. The velocity of the river current is but one tenth of a mile off Ten Hills Farm, but, united with the ebb, it becomes six tenths, — a force equal to the scouring away of sand and ordinary gravel. The same land stream resisting the flood, reduces the force of the latter to four tenths, — a power incapable of overcoming the inertia of gravel, and, therefore, unable to undo the work of the ebb.

If we calculate the work executed in a given time, — a half tidal day, for instance, — by determining the resultant power, on the supposition that all the forces act simultaneously, we shall have the following as the relative results : —

Off	Charlestown,	assumed to be	1.
"	Ten Hills	becomes	1.
Under	Medford Bridge	"	11.
At	Herring Weir	"	8.
"	Wood's Mill	"	14.

The greatest scouring power is exerted at Wood's Mill, upon a bottom of gravel and small shingle. At Herring Weir, a similar bottom is found. At Medford, a gas-pipe forms a solid dam. At Ten Hills, mud is found, except in the centre of the channel, where the bottom is gravelly.

Our conclusion in the special case of the Mystic, it will be remembered, is derived from observations made at the season the least favorable to the complete display of the relation between the upper and lower Mystic, in all its value.

A considerable portion of those large masses of mud lands, which are found in all such places, are deposited on the top of the flood tide, and especially at those periods when the agitation of the water, under the influence of violent winds, disturbs the bottom and sides of the channel. The lighter material is carried upon the shoal ground to the highest level attained by the tide, where the water becomes quiet, and the currents of the ebb have but little appreciable velocity, and no determinate direction.

The current of the ebb, therefore, carries back only a part of the material. Every successive tide, for a certain time, increases in this manner (however slowly), these banks of mud that are to be seen wherever the tide flows. Now, the freshes and the tides of the syzygies, and particularly at the equinoxes, have great influence in remedying this evil; and this influence is especially beneficial when the freshes concur with the most powerful spring tides.

During the lowest stage of a river, the power of the flood may *possibly* be superior to that of the ebb increased by the fresh water, and aided by the inclination of the bed; but, on the other hand, during the freshes and high tides, the power of the flood is far inferior to that of the ebb increased by the fresh water.

The ordinary ebbs would not be able to preserve the lower channels, if they were not assisted by freshes and extraordinary tides.

And the two latter not only act with an immediately beneficial effect upon the lower channels, but they keep open the upper reservoir, and make it a more perfect receptacle for the tide water, which acts with a proportionately greater scouring power, on its return to the sea.

If the water of the rivers did not, in this manner, combine with the ebb tide, or in other words, if, for any reason whatever, the flow of the river were arrested, the channel below the obstruction would be very soon, by the action of the sea, filled up, and the river bed would become a place for cultivation.

This has been exemplified in a remarkable way, in the river Somme.

A lateral canal was constructed along this river from Abbeville to Saint Valery. This canal being sufficiently large to carry off the waters of the river, it was thought advisable to build a dyke in the neighborhood of Abbeville, and divert the waters from their

natural course.   The filling up of the bed of the
Somme was an almost immediate consequence of these
arrangements.

But let us consider the effect of the tides in a channel like that of the Mystic, independently of the
waters of the river.   We have already said that the
ordinary flood tide leaves behind it a portion of its
sedimentary matter.

But under the most unfavorable circumstances, the
ebb current will carry back with it a great part of the
alluvial mud.   This current may not be. entirely efficacious in maintaining the channel in its best state,
but it is efficacious to a certain extent.

If we suppose the waters of the flood to be arrested,
and become stagnant, after having attained their
greatest height, the whole of the matter held in sus-
pension would be deposited.   This stagnation of the
waters of the flood will be, in a measure, brought
about by the construction of a dam at a point below
the point of highest ascent of the tide water.   The
current of the flood will be stopped by this barrier, —
the water will be brought to a state of repose, the
state most favorable to deposit.

When retiring on the ebb, it will acquire no appreciable velocity until it has reached some distance below
the dam.   In this space, it will not have sufficient force
to remove the mud, and a deposition will consequently
take place, even during the ebb ; and the filling up
will be very much more rapid than if the dam did not
exist.

The loss of the navigation of the channel will follow ·
as an immediate consequence.   This is exemplified

again, in the filling up of the channel below the obstruction of the Little Vay, of which we shall say a word directly.

In the adoption of what is called the "lower level," in the Report of Messrs. Baldwin and Stevenson, we have to consider the effect upon both the upper and the lower part of the river, of the proposed dam.

Wherever a dam, bridge, or weir has been built across a river, it has been observed that the alluvial deposits, whether of sand or mud, brought up by the flood, accumulate very rapidly, — particularly in the neighborhood of the obstruction ; and in this way, a quick and sensible diminution of water capacity takes place. The effect is sometimes counteracted in a measure, by freshes, or by the action of equinoctial spring tides.

It is, however, only for a time ; navigation is soon materially injured, if not altogether destroyed.. During the dry season of the year, the return on the ebb of the waters brought in by the flood — the action of the river itself at this season being small—is the principal part of the force by which the channel is kept open. If a bar opposes the progress of the flood tide, the waters, brought to a state of sluggishness, leave their burden in the channel.

We have satisfactory and conclusive evidences, on a larger scale, of the effects of these kinds of interruptions in the rivers Aure and Vire, in the department of Calvados.

The latter, leaving the interior, enters the Bay of Vays, where it winds through sand and mud for a distance of about seven and a half miles. About one third of the way down the bay, it receives the River Aure, which comes from another part of the same department. The Aure was first barred by two bridges with flood-gates, constructed in the town of Isigny, and M. Lejeune, the engineer-in-chief employed in building a quay wall, proved that the existence of these obstructions had diminished the depth of the river in front of the town, below the bridge, by about three feet. Subsequently to this, the River Vire was obstructed by a bridge with flood-gates, called the Bridge of the Little Vay, and after some years, the channel of the bay had altered to such a degree that it was found impossible to reach the port of Isigny, except in vessels of reduced tonnage.

During the spring tide of 1840, there were only five feet of water at full sea at the entrance of the port, and vessels of small draught found it impossible to enter.

For reasons not given, it was decided not to remove the obstructions built upon the Aure; but as there existed no objection to removing the bridge of Vay, for the purpose of opening the pass to the bay, and rendering the approaches to Isigny more convenient, the question was submitted to the Council of the *Ponts et Chaussèes*.

The Council adopted this course, and gave a sketch of the opinions which the consideration of the subject had called forth.

The administration of the *Ponts et Chaussées* had previously adopted this view, when in 1816 it abandoned the project of obstructing the River Scorff, above the Port of Lorient, by a bridge with flood-gates.

M. Lamblardie, the younger, showed that this work,

by cutting off the receptacles above, would lead to the rapid filling up of the channel, and this, by depriving it of the flow of the waters introduced by the flood into the upper reaches. The work had been commenced, and the bridge was constructed over one half the breadth of the stream, when the rapid deposition of alluvium below brought the Council to the unanimous conclusion that it was necessary to arrest the evil.

M. Cordier relates that before the establishment of the sluice in the rear of the port of Dunkirk, the sea entered twice a day, overflowed the vast plain of Waltéringues, and twice retreated. In this manner, the port was traversed twice a day by an immense current, which opened the channel, and maintained the passes of the roadstead.

Since the construction of this sluice, the natural scour has ceased; the deposits have closed the entrance of the harbor; the beach, extending itself more and more, has become continuous, and the passes of the roadstead have contracted. The same results have taken place at Gravelines; the sea formerly ascended to Saint Omer (the resort of vessels), and covered twice a day a plain of several square leagues in extent.

The channel of Gravelines was kept in a good condition, and the creek at the foot of the sand hills at Gravelines was preserved by the natural scour; the navigation of both ports was improved.

The sluices of Gravelines have changed this state of things; the sea has been kept out, the channel has filled up with mud, and this port, formerly a very valuable one, is almost abandoned.

What we have already said goes to show, that the

loss of the port of Isigny was owing to the existence of the bridge, with flood-gates, of the Little Vay; after having, however, cited valuable opinions that directly sustain our own views, we will notice others not less valuable, which might seem, at the first glance, to be opposed to us.

We allude here, particularly, to the use of dykes and jetties in improving the navigation of rivers, examples of which are frequent in Great Britain and on the Continent.

The example of the Seine is brought to our notice in connection with a discussion which took place at the time it was proposed to construct a dyke at its mouth; and in this same class of improvements enter several of the English rivers, such as the Clyde, the Tay, and the Dee.

But M. de Prony, in his memoir, has drawn the distinction between transversal obstructions, like the bridge of the Little Vay, or the proposed dam of the Mystic, which impede the natural flow of the waters of a tidal river, and those jetties, which, being designed to limit the capacity of a channel, add to the condition of being submerged, that of being so placed as to give a special direction to the downward flow.

Speaking of the jetty at the mouth of the Seine, he describes it as being in some sort a prolongation of the shore of the Continent. If, on the contrary, the jetty in question was placed two leagues above the mouth, and was similar in its character to those we have condemned, the part of the Seine comprised between the jetty and the mouth would rapidly fill up. M. de Prony, speaking of the plan of M. Sénéchal

4

says: "M. Sénéchal places his jetty at 9,000 metres (29,528 feet) above the position adopted by M. Pattu, and it would no longer fulfil the condition we have previously mentioned of being a prolongation of the coast of Calvados," (similar in character to Mr. Walker's piers at the entrance of the River Tyne.) "If carried into execution it would leave an indent deeper and more extensive than that in front of the jetty of M. Pattu. In this case, the ascending tide would leave there its alluvial burden. M. Sénéchal was far from denying this effect himself, and, to avoid the difficulty, he furnished his jetty with flood-gates."

These opinions of M. de Prony are cited from the report on the bridge of the Vay, of the Council of the *Ponts et Chaussées,* which report concludes with the declaration that what has been said of the Seine, applies to the Vire, and to all other rivers. In consequence of this report, an order was given to the engineers of Calvados, to remove the gates of the bridge of the Vay, and to let the waters of the sea enter the valley of the Vire.

This order was executed; and the force of the current not only cleared out again the passes of the Vay, but also opened a new bed for the Vire, over ground, which, though of modern formation, had already begun to acquire some consistence. It was observed that the result of the improvements was to restore to navigation the facilities it enjoyed before the construction of the bridge of the Vay.

We might bring forward other examples of the injury done to rivers and their navigation, by means of bars placed within the reach of the tidal water; but our views are sufficiently illustrated.

Having shown what effect the damming of the Mystic will have upon the beds of the river and estuary, we shall pass to the third head of our Report, in which we are to point out the connection between the estuary and the harbor.

RELATION OF THE RIVER AND ESTUARY, TOGETHER WITH THEIR AFFLUENTS, TO BOSTON HARBOR.

We have already, under the preceding head, made some incidental remarks touching upon this topic, particularly where we spoke of the effect produced by the Mystic and a portion of its tributaries upon the times of the tidal currents off Charlestown; these remarks we need not repeat.

The whole inquiry under our present head ought to be satisfactorily answered by simply stating the relation that exists between the harbor and the Mystic; a relation at once of reciprocity and dependence; of reciprocity, arising from the mutual interchange, twice a day, of the tidal waters of the ocean, retarded or accelerated by the land waters; and of dependence on the part of the harbor, because the Mystic is one of the two inner receptacles, or reservoirs, without which the present capacity of Boston Harbor could not be maintained.

Tidal harbors, like that of Boston, owe their preservation to the basin or basins in their rear, in a degree varying with the size of the rivers, or streams, which find through them their channel to the sea.

If there is no river, as in the case of Portland, the harbor is wholly dependent upon the interior basin. But where there is a river, which is a receptacle for tidal water, and at the same time possesses an independent maintaining power, the relation of the interior basin loses some of its importance. This is the case, also, where there is a double opening to the sea.

It would be easy to draw from the Atlantic and Gulf coasts of the United States, examples of the various kinds of harbors that are peculiar to alluvial shores; of tidal harbors that, having no interior basin or reservoir, are fast hastening to decay; of such as depend upon interior basins, exclusively, for their preservation; of tidal harbors, which owe their existence and maintenance to interior reservoirs and rivers combined; and of harbors, which have no regular or influential tides, and are simply the outlets of rivers.

Boston Harbor belongs to the third of the classes above enumerated.

The reservoirs and rivers inside it and above it constitute the original sources of its existence, and the efficient means of its preservation. If they are taken away or diminished, Boston Harbor is taken away or diminished.

In the first division of our second Report on Boston Harbor, we offered you a precise and definite illustration of this view. Under the head of *The Confluence of the Charles and Mystic*, we remarked that "the main features of this division have been preserved; an increase of depth has been effected in a North and South direction, by the removal of a large surplus of 675,000 cubic yards. At the mouth of the Mystic, we find the channel improved by the removal of 449,000 cubic yards, which include a bar seen in Map No. 1, as well as a general deepening of the channel."

And under the head of *Narrows*, also, we noticed the removal of a large amount of deposit on the East Boston shore, which removal, while it was a natural consequence of the diversion of the current of that side, proves, at the same time, the power of the current. And again, under the head of *South Boston Flats, and Main Ship Channel*, we mentioned another removal of deposit, which had benefited the shore of East Boston. A simple inspection of comparative Map No. 4, will enable you to trace the influence of these combined streams in the new channel which they have scooped out for themselves, down even into the mouth of Fort Point Channel.

It might be said, and truly said, that the old channel of the inner harbor affords as satisfactory an evidence as the new one, of the mutual relation and dependence existing between itself and the estuaries above it. Undoubtedly it does afford the same proof; and this brings us back to the first observation under this head, that the whole inquiry ought to be satisfactorily answered by a simple statement of this relation and dependence. In fact, it carries us back to that fundamental principle laid down by the first Commissioners on Boston Harbor, appointed in 1835, "all engineers of eminent scientific attainments," in language that cannot be improved either in perspicuity or simplicity. But a novel force seems to be given to the illustration, a fresh elucidation of the subject seems to have taken place, when we see the waters of the Charles and Mystic compelled, by artificial means, to abandon a portion of their former bed, executing, in a comparatively short space of time, a task corresponding to that capacity and power which had been previously assigned to them.

We have endeavored to give an idea of the comparative work, or scouring power exerted at different places in the Mystic, by combining the periods and velocities of the ebb tide. If we multiply the figures expressing the results by the sectional areas at each place, we shall obtain the relative momenta. Taking the section off Charlestown to be unity, as before, we have : —

Off Charlestown	-	-	-	1.
Off Ten Hills -	-	-	-	0.08
Under Medford Bridge	-	-	-	0.09
At Herring Weir	-	-	-	0.08
At Wood's Mill	-	-	-	0.10

We may conclude, then, that although the action upon a given area of the channel-bed at Wood's Mill is fourteen times as great as that for the same area at the station off Charlestown, the tidal power which would be exerted in a given time, were every water particle in both cases in contact with the channel-bed, is but one tenth as great in the former as in the latter instance.

The attempt might be made, perhaps has been made, to underrate the value of the Mystic by a comparison like the above, which is eminently partial and fanciful. This view of the relations of one part of the harbor to several parts of the interior basin taken separately, presents a comparative estimate, accurate in its facts so far as they are stated, but inaccurate in its omission of other facts equally significant, and indis-

pensable to an entire and comprehensive statement of
the whole subject. We do not, however, admit that any
just argument tending to depreciate the importance of
the estuary and river, could be derived from this comparison, meagre and circumscribed as it is. The case
involves a fundamental principle, into which the question of more or less does not enter, except through
that subtilty of argumentation which aims to gain its
point by means of excessive refinement, or by the
assumption of an extreme quantity. But we will not
give more time than is necessary to a course of reason-
ing that exceeds the true limits of the inquiry. The
following numbers, which we introduce without further
preamble, will serve to show the importance of the
tide waters of the Mystic Reservoir to the inner harbor
of Boston.

1. The area from Charles River Bridge to Chelsea
Bridge, and to the Narrows, is	-	-	398 acres.

2. Of the Mystic Reservoir	-	-	480	"

3. Of 1, with the addition of the Narrows, 584	"

So that the surface of the tidal reservoir of the Mystic
is actually greater than that of the space between
Charles River Bridge, Chelsea Bridge, and the Narrows,
and nearly equal to that space, with the addition of the
Narrows.

4. The surface of the tidal prism between high and
low water within the same limits as in 1, is	80 acres.

5. Of the tidal prism of Mystic River,	480	"

6. Of the tidal prism, as in 3,	91	"

So that the Mystic Reservoir tidal surface is more than
five times the corresponding surface of the inner harbor
between Charles River Bridge, Chelsea Bridge, and the

Narrows inclusive, bringing into strong relief the value of the Mystic flats and meadows overflowed at high water.

7. The cubic contents of tide water (the tidal prism within the limits specified in 1) are 5,770,000 cubic yds.

8. The cubic contents of the
Mystic River tide water are -   -   8,410,000   "   "

9. The cubic contents of the part of the inner harbor specified in 3, including the Narrows, are -   8,710,000   "   "

It certainly is not needful to subjoin to this comparative statement a recommendation that nothing be done for any purpose, or under any pretext whatever, permanently to impair the usefulness of the Mystic Reservoir; or, should this be thought expedient, we certainly may spare ourselves the trouble of elaborating an argument, or uttering by anticipation a complaint. We have endeavored to give our views in a manner at once intelligible, and free from the liability of misapprehension. If we appear, by the form in which we have presented them, to advocate their adoption, it has been the natural result of strong convictions, and not of partial motives or feelings.

General Remarks.

The preceding part of this Report possesses the character of an essay, or series of notes with conclusions, which it has been thought advisable to arrange under separate heads, in order more fully to show the method and connection pervading them. We shall pursue a similar course in what remains to be said,. though for a different reason. The topics still to be treated are somewhat desultory, though all having a direct bearing upon the main inquiry contained in your order of the 23d of January. This bearing we are careful to define, pointing out distinctly the precise place which each one of our separate discussions is designed to occupy in the general views or plan of this Report. The subdivisions under this general head are as follows: —   .

a — *Estuary as a Reservoir.*

b — *Reservation of the Mystic Pond Waters, and employment of Sluices, or Flood-gates.*

c — *Mr. Stevenson's View.*

d — *Mystic Lower Pond as a Reservoir.*

e — *Characteristics of the Mystic and other Ponds.*

f — *Recapitulation.*

a — *Estuary as a Reservoir.* The views concerning the reservoir given under the third head, at the end, really require no corroborative testimony or support; yet, to elucidate the subject, and to satisfy the general judgment, we will cite some instances and authorities in point, showing the disadvantages that have resulted from preventing the " tidal inflow," or the " inflowing of more than ordinary tides," into the rivers, and inner and

5

upper reservoirs of tidal harbors, and the conclusions to which distinguished inquirers have been carried by the most systematic and thorough research.

The Commissioners on Tidal Harbors, appointed by Royal Commission, in April, 1844, say, in the prefatory remarks of their first Report : " We find that very great and increasing injury to the best interests of the country has accrued from negligence of the several authorities in permitting the improper removal of soil and beach, as well as by *embankments, weirs, and other obstructions of a similar nature, which check the free flow of the tide, impair its strength, and thus permanently diminish the general depth of the river*. And, on the other hand, that when the aid of experience and science has been called in, and a due vigilance has been exercised, a proportionate improvement has been invariably the result." And it cites the following instances as cases in point.

It is given as a reason for the tardy improvement of the River Clyde, " that weirs have been permitted across the river, nay, sanctioned by Act of Parliament (49 Geo. III, cap. 74), so as to prevent the flow of the tide above the city, and stop all navigation above the bridges," and " that a considerable expense for dredging might have been saved, if the natural flow of the tidal water had been properly directed."

Again, in speaking of the River Blyth and harbor of Southwold, it says : "As a general, although not universal principle, no cause has operated more extensively to injure the entrances of harbors throughout the United Kingdom, than excluding the tidal waters from lands below the level of high water, which served as natural reservoirs for the flood tide, and were the means

of affording a valuable scouring power during the ebb.
Nor does any subject more deserve the vigilant attention of your Majesty's Government, or of those intrust-
ed with the conservancy of our harbors, than such
encroachments, which are usually made quietly and
gradually, and, when once completed, are difficult after-
wards to remove.

"We have thought it right to enter into the above
details, since Southwold is entirely dependent upon
tidal waters for existence as a port, and since the value
of the daily tidal scour in all our harbors does not seem
to be sufficiently appreciated; nor can any case more
strongly prove the duty of jealously guarding against
similar encroachments."

And again in the case of Rye Harbor.

"For several miles round the town of Rye, and
immediately adjacent to the harbor, there are large
tracts of marsh land, a greater part of which are owned
by proprietors residing in the neighborhood. Over a
great portion of this plain the sea was formerly
accustomed to flow at every tide, and thus formed a
considerable back water, which operated as a scour to
the harbor of Rye, and kept the channel open. The
proprietors, however, uncontrolled by any guardian of
the port, began by degrees to exclude the tide, and
no steps being taken to restrain their encroachments,
they obtained an Act of Parliament, erected dams and
sluices across the river a short distance above the town,
and finally excluded the tidal waters.

"By these means hundreds of acres of marsh have
been reclaimed; while the harbor, deprived of its back
waters, yielded to the mass of sand and shingle which

rolled in with every wave, and which have now nearly obliterated the appearance of a channel.

"Three rivers drain this tract of country, and had there been no obstructions in their channels, they would have afforded an ample reservoir for tidal waters." (*Rennie's Rep.*)

The same Commissioners, in their second Report on tidal harbors, enumerate other instances equally important and instructive.

The harbor of Cork, for example, was injured by the "seven weirs that crossed the River Leed within one and a half miles of Cork; and again at Sligo, weirs exist which obstruct the upward flow of the tide."

And again at Belfast, "the lower lock of the Logan navigation is only one and a half miles above the town, and thus prevents the upward flow of the tide," to the injury of the harbor.

And again upon the Dee, "a weir or milldam, rising eleven feet above the bed of the river, exists just above the city, dams the water up for several miles, and prevents the upward flow of the tide;" and this is mentioned as one of the sources of the injury to the Dee.

And again Exeter is injured by the South Devon Railway, which has diminished the estuary and excluded the tidal water; and again at Newcastle, complaints are made of Newcastle Bridge, which, "with its narrow arches, heavy piers, and additional starling, acts almost as a milldam;" and again at Whitby, "a milldam which stops the upward flow of the tide, and a railway dam, recently made, which excludes 30,000 cubic yards of water on every spring tide," are referred to as a means of injury to the harbor.

And finally, at Yarmouth, "the narrowness of Yarmouth Bridge, and of the adjoining part of the haven," are spoken of as injurious to the harbor, because they act as a "great impediment to the flow of the tide."

We shall cite one more distinguished *authority*, — that of the Commissioners on the Tyne. In their summary report of May, 1859, they say : —

" It would appear probable that it is the daily ebb and flow of the waters from the sea that principally maintain undiminished the width and depth of that part which may be termed the estuary, and which regularly scours the channel within its reach ; it is, therefore, of the greatest consequence to admit and properly direct the largest possible quantity of tidal water.

" Although *this is admitted by all whose opinion is of value*," &c.

It remains to be observed that the Commissioners on tidal harbors were invested with authority to call before them all persons from whom they could obtain information, suited to the purposes of the Commission, and to administer oaths to persons under examination ; and that, in pursuance of this authority, they summoned the most distinguished engineers, both in the civil and public services ; and especially those men (it is not worth while to enumerate their names) who have taken the most conspicuous part in the construction, improvement, preservation, and rescue of tidal harbors.

Even the least interested are aware that there have been some signal examples of successful engineering in the rivers and harbors of Great Britain during the

present century; and it is very desirable that the principles by which this success was secured should be
better understood. Persons who speak with authority
sometimes cite the examples of Havre and Dieppe, or
of the Tyne, Clyde, &c., without, perhaps, a well-digested
knowledge of the distinctive peculiarities of these harbors, of the objects of improvement, or of the modes in
which those objects are accomplished.

It is upon the opinions of the distinguished and successful engineers referred to that the conclusions of the
Commission, which we have quoted above, are based.

*b — Reservation of the Mystic Pond Waters, and employ-
ment of Sluices, or Flood-gates.* The observations contained
in this branch of our subject are *partly* called forth by
the following sentences in the *Report for supplying the
City of Charlestown with pure water :* —

" Another and important advantage arising from the
use of these sluices will be the ability to scour and keep
clean the bed of the Mystic River, preventing the 'silt-
ing up' so common to all tidal rivers, thereby improving
this stream for navigable purposes. Samples, on a
large scale, of sluices, constructed expressly for sweep-
ing away at low water the accumulating deposits, are
found in the most important tidal harbors on the English
and French coasts; and were it not for some effectual
remedy of this kind, many of the most important would
have been long since completely silted up." (pp. 35, 36.)

From the language here employed, taken in connection with some other sources of information, we
learn that Dieppe, Havre, and similar ports, are the examples referred to in the *Report.*

We will take from M. Élie de Beaumont his concise

and accurate description of the entrance of the valley of the Béthune at Dieppe.

On each side of the entrance of the Béthune which leads to the port of Dieppe, there are two cliffs of chalk, of considerable elevation.

The town is situated upon low ground protected by a natural sea-wall *(levèe de galet)*, which extends to the entrance of the port. The sea disturbs the stones of this wall, and tends to force them in a certain direction, which is most frequently that from West to East, because the prevailing winds are in this direction, and because the waves that break upon the shore in bad weather have in general a line of direction from West to East.

Hence arose the necessity for constructing very solid jetties, which project beyond the sea-wall, for the purpose of preventing the stones from filling the entrance of the port.

Notwithstanding this protection, the shingle sometimes gets by the jetty, and fills up the entrance. No better means of freeing a channel has been discovered than that of keeping back, by means of a basin, the waters of the river swollen by the tide. The gates are opened at low water, and a very rapid current *(une Chasse)* flows out, which carries a part of the shingle into the sea.

This means is employed in many ports, liable to similar obstructions: it is very expensive, and is a proof of the greatness of those natural forces with which the engineers have to contend in order to keep the entrance of such harbors in a practicable state.

M. Bailleul, in the beginning of his memoir on the

port of Havre (1838), says: The port of Havre is assailed by two powerful enemies, the débris (shingle) of cliffs (on the sea-coast of Normandy between Etretat and Havre) and the silt (alluvium) of the Seine, which combine in their efforts to block up the port, and will succeed in doing it if a remedy is not soon applied.

It has been admitted, observes M. Lamblardie, in a remarkable memoir on the coasts of Haute-Normandie, published in Havre in 1789, that the coast suffers every year a loss by degradation of about one foot throughout its whole extent.

If then we allow that the distance from Cape Antifer to Cape de la Hêve is 13.67 miles (25,000 metres), and that the mean height of the Cliffs exceeds one hundred and sixty feet, we shall find that we are below the truth in estimating at 523,200 cubic yards (400,000 cubic metres) the material of all sorts, sand, marl, and flint, which the sea carries annually into the little road up the entrance of the port, and to the shoals of the same.

These materials are placed at the disposal of the currents, which take them up from the feet of the cliffs in great quantities after thaws, heavy rains, and violent storms.

It was to remedy this evil that *écluses de chasse* (sluices) were resorted to at Havre (in connection with jetties), in the beginning of the last century. It was for the same purpose, and to meet the same difficulty, that the great *écluses de chasse* were constructed about 1780, in the ports of Dieppe, Saint Valery, and Freport (pp. 1, 2, 11, 12).

It is wholly unnecessary to enter into a detailed

comparison in order to show that these descriptions of artificial ports, opening upon an external sea-coast, and exposed to obstruction at their entrance by coarse drift detached from neighboring cliffs in storms, and transported by currents and ocean waves, bear no resemblance whatever to the protected and secluded Mystic, pursuing its undisturbed course in its natural alluvial channel, and discharging its waters into a sheltered bay.

But the above quotations from the Report contain what we conceive to be misconceptions upon the subject of river improvements, which would be mischievous if carried into practice, and against the injurious consequences of which, the public mind should, if possible, be guarded.

A plan which includes violent and sudden changes is wholly opposed to the fundamental principle which lies at the bottom of all improvements of tidal rivers.

A letter addressed to one of our number by Mr. Charles L. Stevenson, civil engineer, and intended for the consultation of the Commission, furnishes us with the occasion for treating the reservation of the waters of the Mystic, and the use of sluices, in a more specific manner, and with special reference to the case in hand.

c — *Mr. Stevenson's view* is presented in the following extract from his letter : —

" If the fresh waters flowing from Mystic Pond be retained in the pond during such hours as recent investigations indicate that the tidal inflow up the river would be thereby increased by an amount nearly equal to the volume of the fresh water yield, or as much less as may be found most advisable, a sufficient amount of water for Charlestown or Chelsea may be diverted, *and the balance of retained fresh water thrown in in aid of the increased tidal waters at such time of the ebb as experience and investigation show it to be of most benefit to the river, this will admit of as complete, if not better and surer scouring action than at present.*

"In the making a tidal reservoir of that space, now occupied by the fresh-water flow from the pond, may we not so far imitate nature in the action observable in tidal reservoirs as to expect like results? Let us suppose Mystic Pond raised, as proposed for the ' High Level,' (*Vide* Water Report, B. & S.) or some six feet higher than at present, with a dam at its outlet near Weir Bridge, so as to make it a fresh-water reservoir. The average fresh-water yield of the pond in 1859 was estimated at 23¼ million gallons per day ; when acting as a storage reservoir we may safely assume the available yield at all times to equal twenty million gallons, or ten million for each tide. The maximum amount of water required for Charlestown and Chelsea, estimating for 100,000 persons, is six million gallons per day, or three million for twelve hours ; this leaves some seven million gallons *with six feet head available to increase the tidal flow down the river at every ebb.* If we suppose the flow from Mystic Pond stopped, so that none of the water flowing therefrom remains in the bed of the river, above the estuary, at the commencement of flood at that point, the tidal flow up the river will be increased by an amount equal to the retained fresh water ; or, taking a similar tide to that of Oct. 3, as an example, some nine million gallons more of tidal water would have passed into the river at each tide. *Having some seven million gallons of water in addition to this, under control, with a head of six feet, it would seem that the proposed erections, so far from being detrimental, would enable us much more completely to conserve the channel, as far, at least, as the head of the estuary, as the loss now due to the meeting of the flood and ebb currents is avoided, while we have it in our power to increase the velocity of the ebb, and the quantity of water that is of value, if at any time desirable.*"

The italics in the preceding extract from Mr. Stevenson's paper are our own. We have employed them to distinguish to the eye of the reader, the passages to which we desire to call his particular attention. Mr. Stevenson's letter is to be found in the Appendix.

The substitution of an artificial dam in the place of the natural dam, and above the latter, is in itself not only admissible, argues Mr. Stevenson, but even desirable for the maintenance and improvement of the river bed, apart from other considerations. The artificial dam will serve an economical purpose, and the loss of the water taken for daily use will be more than supplied by the increased range given to the tide of flood; but this last is not the question we are discussing. The question we are discussing is the benefit to be conferred upon the bed of the Mystic River, and by transmission upon Boston Harbor, by the judicious employment of flood-gates or sluices at the outlet of Mystic Pond.

We make this distinction, not for the purpose of adding anything to the clearness of Mr. Stevenson's statement, but in order to define the limit of application of a few of the thoughts that are suggested by the perusal of his paper, and presented here.

Let us inquire into the effects likely to follow from a reservation of the Mystic Pond waters, during the period of flood-current in the harbor, and the subsequent sluicing off during the ebb.

Since the increase of head in the Mystic Ponds that would result from a retention of the waters during six hours could not greatly exceed that now caused by the rise of the tide, we may safely assume that the average flow of the water discharged during the ebb would be about a mean of the rates observed at those points in the river at which the stream now pursues its natural course.

	Miles per hour.
The mean velocity of downward current at Wood's Mill Station was found to be about	1.30
At Herring Weir	1.00
At Ten Hills	0.60
At Station in Estuary of Mystic River (one mile above Charlestown Dry Dock)	0.44

The average of these is 0.83 miles per hour. The total distance between the extreme stations of our list exceeds six miles. From this estimate of the rate of travel for the Mystic Pond waters, it appears evident that under ordinary circumstances, no portion of their scouring power can be transmitted to the lower part of the Mystic River during the entire fall of the tide ; but that the greater portion of the water released by raising the gates at the time proposed, must, long before it reaches the harbor, conflict with the incoming flood current. Again; if by constructing a dam at the outlet of the ponds, the excess of rain-falls of the winter months could be stored up, so that a general increase over the present head of water could be insured for the entire year, no considerable quickening of the current at the *Estuary* would occur during the period of letting off. We have shown in the first part of this Report that the great increase of the sectional area in the lower portions of the river, as contrasted with the contracted and shallow channel above, causes a very great exhaustion of the power of the waters of Mystic Pond before they reach the place where this power can be most useful. The fresh-water current slackens so suddenly on reaching the broader and deeper waters, that even were the surface of the Mystic Pond six or ten feet above its present level, we doubt if, when suddenly discharged, it would augment the velocity of the ebb current in the Estuary more than two tenths of a mile. The Mystic Ponds are too distant to be made very useful as sluicing reservoirs while the channel connecting them with the sea is so very tortuous and shallow.

There is one circumstance connected with the use of sluices which has always been found highly unfavorable; it is this, that the greatest expenditure of power is in the immediate neighborhood of the sluice-way; and in the case of the Mystic, the scour would be mostly expended upon a bed of gravel and stones, which it would no doubt sweep down the river until these materials reached the deeper, and consequently more important portions of the stream, where the current, abating its force, would relinquish them. Even now this process may be seen at the periods of freshet, the gravel and stones are rolled along the bed of the stream, and at last come to rest, forming ridges, or bars.

We hold that, as far as possible, a uniformity of motion in a stream should be preserved ; and that, if power is to be artificially communicated, its operation should be suited to give a moderate velocity to a great mass of water, rather than to convert small streams into torrents.   •

In the useful action of inland waters for the maintenance of harbors, it is not a necessary condition that the river stream shall flow from the interior to the sea during a single ebb tide, or in a single day, but simply that there shall be a seaward gain in the resultant motion given to earthy particles by the abrasion of the water, and that a sufficient mass of water shall be set in motion to prevent an abrupt exhaustion of power on reaching the sea. It is a remarkable fact that some of the most rapid rivers have the shallowest bars at their embouchures. The immediate loss of head, and enlargement of section, which a mountain stream experiences on reaching the sea renders it powerless to bear forward into deep waters the gravel and sand which its previous strength has enabled it so easily to sweep down from the uplands. *It is not by sudden violence that Nature executes her best offices, but by persistence in gentle efforts.*

What we have said concerning sluices in the two last sections, whether general or special, may very properly be brought to a termination by citing the judgment of Mr. G. R. Runnel as to their real utility.

" The history of such ports as Dover, Folkestone,

Newhaven, Fécamp, Brighton, Dieppe, Havre, and Ostend, demonstrates the inefficiency of sluices.

"In the French ports, so strongly does the conviction of the inutility of sluicing prevail, that the engineers have almost entirely abandoned it." (*Rud. of Hydraulic Engineering*, pp. 88, 89.)

d — Mystic Pond, as a Reservoir. In the second Report on Boston Harbor, which we have recently transmitted to you, we pointed out some changes of vital importance that had taken place in the reservoirs, and promised that when all our materials were collected and digested, we would endeavor to designate the precautions necessary to guard against similar encroachments in future. It was not our intention then, neither is it now, to express an unavailing regret that so large a quantity of the tidal marshes and mud lands should have been filled during the present century. This operation was the concomitant of the growth of the city ; and indeed, to a certain extent, the very mode of its prosperity and increase.

The political economists of the day would not have hesitated to sanction and encourage the schemes of enterprising and sagacious projectors, even if they had foreseen that one of their results would be the loss of water capacity in the harbor. Their part was to lay the foundations of commercial greatness ; the duty devolved upon us is to maintain and improve the instruments of commerce ; and with prudent measures, it will always be possible to secure to the port of Boston its present reputation of being one of the safest and most commodious harbors in the world.

Of these prudent measures, one of the most obvious, and least difficult, is the improvement of old, or the formation of new, tidal reservoirs. Now Mystic Pond, if opened to the free ingress of the tide, would prove a most valuable source of power; the currents of the harbor would then be quickened, their domain extended seaward, and Mystic River converted into a navigable arm of the sea.

In the central portions of the harbor, the tidal currents have peculiar values as positive scouring agents, for here the flood and ebb drifts do not traverse a common path, as in the narrow reaches of the Mystic River, and therefore cannot cancel each other's efforts. The islands divide the currents into different streams, and in such a manner that the ebbs and floods are not reciprocals of each other. The forms of the islands are very irregular, their outer or seaward shores lie at different angles, and present different outlines from those on the inside ; so that the flood and ebb currents, impinging upon these obstacles, do not suffer similar deflections or interferences, and are, therefore, compelled to pursue independent paths. The fine channels on either side of the Lower Middle, examined during the past season, offer excellent illustrations of the benefits that may result from the conditions to which we have referred. Of these two channels, that lying to the southward of the rocky shoal is maintained by the *ebb*, which predominates greatly over the flood in scouring power; while the channel to the northward is the work of the *flood*, the strong and steady action of which presents a marked contrast to the feeble and irregular motion of the ebb. These effects are clearly

traceable to the alternating influences of several islands
upon the courses of the tidal streams.

Boston Harbor owes to its numerous islands, not only
its sheltered and secure anchorages, but many of its
deep and spacious channels. To the destruction of
Bird Island, and the consequent changes in the direc-
tions of the currents, can be traced the accumulation of
certain shoals, as we may show in a future report, when
the Physical Survey of the harbor is completed. But
let us resume our investigation.

The bottom of Mystic Pond lies below the bed of
Broad Sound Channel; it would be itself a spacious
harbor, and is admirably sheltered. Upon Diagram C,
a profile of the natural dam which separates this fine
basin from the harbor may be seen. The portion lying
above the 5.5 feet line on our diagram (mean low water
of the harbor) is about two and a quarter miles in
extent, and six and a half feet in maximum thickness.
Were this barrier reduced by removing about two feet
of the earth for a short distance, there is no doubt that
the natural scour of the powerful ebb and flood streams
would then become sufficient to complete the destruction of the dam. It would require, it is true, skilful
engineering to prevent the natural forces from making
a disadvantageous use of the matter removed; but all
this could be controlled by proper care, and by slow
degrees of progress.

With regard to the ebb and flood currents which
would be induced in the narrow portion of Mystic
River by the proposed cut, we may remark that they
would not be so violent as a comparison of the present
relations of water-heads might indicate; because, by

7

giving a free course to the whole range of the tide *wave*, a portion of the difference of level occurring on either the rise or fall of the tide would be restored, and less current called into action.

We need not go far to illustrate this point. The South Bay, a basin of double the area of the Lower Mystic Pond, is drained and filled by the tides without creating currents of sufficient strength to occasion serious difficulties. The rise and fall of the tides is not necessarily accompanied by currents, for those are only called into action by the *delay* of the wave due to friction, &c. In channels of great depths the tide *wave* propagates itself with such rapidity, that the surface of the sea alters its position but slightly from the horizontal; gravity scarcely suffices to overcome the inertia, friction, and viscosity among the water particles.

Again, it may be asked, what change will take place in the height of Mystic Lower Pond if the river channel is deepened. We have many instances, on our coast, of lagoons communicating with the ocean by narrow inlets, and from observations of the Coast Survey it appears that they preserve nearly the same mean level as the ocean, notwithstanding the very great reduction of range the tide wave undergoes in passing into any of them. If we leave the land waters out of consideration, we may presume that, in order to preserve a natural equilibrium, the *outflow* and *inflow* of a lagoon should be equal. Now, since the velocities of currents vary with the square roots of the heads which engender them, it follows that an equality of ebb and flood currents, at the entrance of a lagoon, will be maintained when the mean water height of this basin

is a plane which cuts the tide wave into two such portions that the sum of the square roots of hourly heights,
measured from this plane during a tidal day, will be
zero.   On the open coast, the symmetrical figure of the
tide wave is everywhere exactly bisected by the plane
which we denominate the mean level of the sea.

The tide wave which passes through an inlet in a
lagoon of very great extent is almost entirely lost. The
Great South Bay, Long Island, is almost tideless ; and
at Fire Island Inlet, which connects this lagoon with
the ocean, the slack-water epochs are half tidal, — that
is, the surface of the inland basin lying nearly at the
mean level of the sea, the water does not flow in from
the ocean till the tide outside has risen about half its
range ; and the flood drift continues till the tide has
fallen again to about the level of the lagoon, after
which ebb commences.   The maximum ebb and flood
drifts occur nearly at times of high and low water.

Although, comparatively speaking, the Lower Mystic
Pond can be transformed into but a small lagoon, there
will be found some trace of the phenomena we have
described.   The tidal range will be less than in the
harbor, and the current epochs will be a little later than
those of the local tide.

It is true that a very great disturbance of the tide
now takes place in the Mystic River, so that even the
upper portion of the wave is disturbed ; but it is believed
that a sufficient deepening of the channel will restore,
in a great degree, the normal form ; or, at least, that
different parts of the tide wave will then suffer corresponding changes, so that its positive and negative portions (considered with regard to the mean sea-level)
may be counterparts of each other.

We may conclude, then, that the mean level of Mystic Lower Pond, if converted into a tidal reservoir, will be about the same as that of the sea, or from four to five feet lower than at present. A considerable rise and fall of the tide will take place, but not so great as that of the harbor.

1.3 $\sqrt{h}$ is the expression which now seems to represent the velocities of the current in the Upper Mystic River, — h being the head, and the constant 1.3 being computed from our observations. By estimating the hourly rise or fall of the pond with the tide of the harbor, — considering this to take place with the *wave propagation*, as well as by *flowing water*, — we cannot see that the average rate of the currents will exceed two miles per hour, or the maximum rate reach above three miles, in the narrower reaches of the channel. If the channel were to be so much enlarged as to allow the passage of a broad section of the tide wave, the level of the pond would rise and fall so nearly with that of the harbor as to occasion only very feeble currents.

If the improvement here proposed be only partially effected by deepening the channel to the level of the river bed at Herring Weir (a little more than four feet above mean low water of the harbor), the mean height at which the surface of the pond would stand would be about two feet below its present level. This estimate is made on the supposition that the bed of the channel will remain fixed, which, considering the increase of scour, is not probable.

The actions of tidal currents, when undisturbed by waves or other variable causes, is to equalize the depths of the bays and channels over which they have free range. *It is, then, of the highest importance to connect any basin with a harbor when the depth of the former exceeds that of the latter.*

c — *Characteristics of the Mystic and certain other Ponds.* The following particulars comprise the leading results of Mr. Mitchell's investigations.

The two Mystic Ponds do not differ greatly in form and depth in the character of their shores, or other features which would strike the casual observer; but our more intimate examinations have led us to the discovery of very important points of distinction. The two basins are separated by a very narrow, though shallow bar, which so perfectly divides their waters as to allow of a marked contrast of chemical and mechanical conditions. The Lower Pond, visited occasionally by the sea, has accumulated a quantity of saline and sulphurous matter, which impregnates the whole mass of water lying below a fixed plane; while the Upper Pond is essentially pure and homogeneous throughout. We should mention here that the existence of foul matter in the Lower Pond is stated in Baldwin and Stevenson's Water Report of 1857.

In Tables 5 and 6 will be found the results of experiments upon the temperatures, specific gravities, etc., of these ponds, and upon Diagram *E*, the same results plotted in curves. These experiments show that in the Lower Pond, at a certain depth from the surface, we pass very suddenly from a warm to a cold stratum, and less suddenly from a rare to a more dense body of water; while, for the upper pond, we have the usual circular variation in the conducted heat, and no considerable variation of specific gravity for different depths.

By the taste and smell, it was observed that in the Lower Pond the upper ten or fifteen feet stratum is fresh; below this, is a narrow belt of odorless salt water, and from a depth of 19½ feet to bottom, is found the very foul matter to which we have referred. Our hydrometers detected the passage from the fresh to the salt, and from the salt to the foul water; but our thermometer gave nearly uniform temperatures for the first two strata.

That the experiments of September 1, given in Table 5, may not be understood to contradict this assertion, we must explain that for the trial made at twenty feet in depth, the deep-sea thermometer, being of some sixteen inches in length, actually rested with portions of its scale in different strata, so that an intermediate result was obtained accidentally.

We have drawn a broken line, connecting the results of this date, upon the Diagram, to indicate that the curve is doubtful.

Still further experiments were made to ascertain the precise limits of the stratum impregnated with sulphur, by suspending metallic bands from floats, and observing the chemical action during different periods of time. Copper bands plated on one side with silver, if allowed to remain suspended twenty-four hours, were found to be completely blackened on the copper side below a point of $19_{\tfrac{9}{10}}$ feet from the surface of the pond, and the line or limit of the sulphuret was sharply defined. When suspended for short periods, the bands showed a steady increase of the sulphuret as the distance below the initial plane increased.

For nearly all our experiments in the Lower Pond, the silver side of the band remained untarnished, but a single experiment made at the very bottom of the pond showed a decided effect upon both sides. Doubtless the galvanic action between the two metals affected our results, for on using thickly-plated wire, we observed that the silver became rapidly sulphuretted. Test tapes, prepared with acetate of lead, and lowered down, and at once drawn up, gave indication of the presence of sulphur. The mud on the bottom was found to be sulphurous only for a limited depth.

In the Upper Pond, all tests failed to reveal the presence of an undue degree of foreign matter in the water. On a single occasion, a piece of plated copper, after lying on the bottom, was found to be tarnished, but nothing impure was observed in the taste or smell of the water or underlying mud.

Spot, Cochituate, Spy, and Fresh Ponds, were examined, but in the last named only could any peculiarities be detected. In Fresh Pond, a stratum of water affecting mostly the silver side of our plated band was found holding an intermediate position, the surface and lowest strata being apparently quite pure. The hydrometer detected no marked changes of density for different depths, and the thermometer showed a uniformity of temperatures below a point near the surface.

In Mystic River, examinations of specific gravities showed a predominance of fresh water as low down as Medford Bridge. It was noticed at this place that the salt water inclined to press up along the bottom on the last of the flood, so that the water near the bed of the stream was found of greater density than that upon the surface. At the Boston and Maine Railroad Bridge, the conditions are more nearly those of the sea than of river water.

Our tables of specific gravities are reduced to the unit for 60° Fahrenheit, so that the surface waters of the ponds may increase their weights as the temperature descends. It is a fact familiarly known, that the maximum density of fresh water is reached at about 40°, and the aggregate change in the specific gravity of water between this and 60° is less than one thousandth; it is evident, therefore, from Table 5, that no interchange of water can take place between the different strata of Mystic Lower Pond ; for even at the depth of eighteen feet, the density, as observed, is much greater than the maximum for the fresh water of the surface. In the Upper Pond, a circulation may gradually go on as the seasons change.

The winter temperatures of Mystic Ponds are given in Table 7, and upon Diagram *F*. These observations were made when the ponds had been frozen over nearly three weeks, and the covering of ice had become about eight inches in thickness.

We may remark of these observations that they indicate the *circulating process* for the Upper Pond, and the *conduction* of heat for the impure portion of the Lower Pond. The sudden change of temperature, as the point of observation passes from the pure to the foul water, is again exhibited by these observations, and at about the same depth as in summer.

In order to complete these investigations, and to procure, for the satisfaction of the City Government, important information, the following inquiries were submitted to the distinguished Rumford Professor in the Scientific School of Harvard University, Mr. Horsford.

1. The amount of saline and mineral matter in general as compared with standard pure water?

2. If an excess of certain ingredients is found, whence their source, — local, or from influx of the sea?

3. If from the sea, do the conditions indicate frequent or rare renewals of sea water?

4. Are the muds strongly impregnated with mineral salts, or other substances, calculated to contaminate spring water long in contact with them?

· His full and detailed reply to these inquiries will be found in the Appendix to this Report; we shall limit ourselves in its text to a quotation of the summary alone.

"The Upper Mystic Pond is throughout its depth an eminently pure and soft water.

"The Lower Mystic Pond water is sufficiently pure at the surface, and for a depth of some fifteen feet, to serve the purpose of domestic use.

"Beyond the depth of eighteen feet, the amount of saline matter is such as to impair the taste, and below twenty feet the presence of sulphurous compounds, offensive to the taste and smell, with increasing saline matter, renders it wholly unfit for use.

"The excess of saline matter is due to the inflow — not infiltration — of sea water, on the occasions of high tide, — how frequently, and in what quantity, hydrographic observations only can determine.

"The foregoing observations are quite in keeping with occasional and rare, rather than frequent supplies

8

of sea water. The sulphurous body at depths below twenty feet, is not due to the decomposition of any mineral constituents in the earth or rock at the bottom or on the sides of the pond. It is not due to the mud at the bottom of the pond spontaneously decomposing in a pure fresh water.

" It is conceived, in part, to be extracted from the muds of Mystic River banks and flats, as the incoming tide flows over them and discharges into the pond; and in part to the reducing action of the organic matter at the bottom of the pond on the sulphates of the sea water with which these organic matters of the mud are saturated.

" The sea water flowing in at high water, by virtue of its superior specific gravity, flows to the lower depths of the pond, displacing the purer, lighter water. The saline water, from the bottom up, diminishes but little in density till a level of forty feet from the surface is attained; from this point up, the diffusion is nearly in inverse ratio to the depth.

"If the sea water were shut out, the law of diffusion would obviously require that in time all the excess of saline matter should be removed. The action of the inflowing current from the Upper Pond would facilitate this purification."

f — Recapitulation. Under the first head of this Report, we entered into an examination of the Mystic Ponds and River, in the course of which we introduced a summary of the observations made by Mr. Henry Mitchell, an assistant in the Coast Survey of the United States, upon the currents, tides, tidal currents, and tide wave of these waters.

Under the second head, we presented the results of this examination with reference to the estuary of the Mystic.

Under the third head, we explained the relation of the river and estuary, together with their affluents, to Boston Harbor.

The object of the investigation, thus far, to which we gave an orderly course, was to ascertain the connection existing between these several parts or places; and having established their interdependence, we found that it would be inexpedient to do anything which would permanently impair the usefulness of the Mystic Reservoir.

Under the last head of our Report, which, in the disposition of its separate topics, was unavoidably desultory, we treated the general importance of interior reservoirs to tidal harbors like Boston; pointed out the manner in which the Mystic Lower Pond might be improved, and be made to perform a valuable office to the lower channels; and combated the idea that a dam with flood-gates at the outlet of Mystic Pond, or across the Mystic River, could be beneficial, or, in fact, could be otherwise than detrimental to the channel below it.

Throughout the whole of our Report, we have distinguished, by putting them in italics, the conclusions resulting from the observations made in the field, and also those general views and fundamental principles already established by former observers, and common to the profession of engineering in tidal harbors.

It must be understood that the intelligent engineer has already arrived at the determination of certain fixed principles of conduct, by means of observations

and experiments ; observations and experiments which
(in the progress of accumulated knowledge) have
ripened into comprehensive generalizations, or into
governing rules for further observations and experiments suited to local circumstances.

We have before observed, but it cannot be too often
repeated, that among these fundamental principles, the
one which holds the primary place consists in the
improvement of the natural and existing state of
things; making it the object to assist nature, and to
use the laws of nature derived from study and observation, either by restraining or promoting her operations, in such a manner as will accomplish the object in
view.

It has been wisely said, in another case, where man
combines and disposes of the operation of natural
laws, in order to modify or improve nature, that he
employs the means which nature herself supplies ;
above that art which adds to nature is an art that
nature makes.

And such has been the general scope and tenor of
this Report. Our calculations and conclusions, the rules
we have laid down, the principles we have enunciated,
have been derived either from observations and experiments instituted for this purpose, or from observations
and experiments made at other times and in other
places belonging to the common treasury of knowledge.
And further, we have taken into view not only immediate, but also distant effects and changes ; regarding
those that affect the prosperity of a future generation,
as not less worthy of our attention than those that
directly concern ourselves.

Our general conclusions are : —

1. That it would be inexpedient to make the "changes contemplated by the City of Charlestown, in the disposition and level of the water in Mystic Pond."

2. That Mystic Lower Pond may be converted into a reservoir with advantage to the channels of the river and harbor.

3. If the *upper* pond is cut off and converted to the use of the towns as proposed in the Report of the Engineers of the City of Charlestown, compensation should be made by such excavations as will secure free tidal flow into the *lower* pond.

We have the honor to be, very respectfully,

Your most obedient servants,

JOS. G. TOTTEN, Bt. Brig. Gen.,
U. S. Engineers.

A. D. BACHE,
Superintendent U. S. Coast Survey.

CHARLES HENRY DAVIS,
Commander U. S. N. Supt. N. A.

To His Honor, F. W. LINCOLN, JR.,
Mayor of Boston.

And,

JESSE HOLBROOK, ESQ.,
Alderman, and Chairman of Harbor Committee, Boston.

TABLES AND DIAGRAMS.

9

TABLES.

TABLE 1.

Mystic River.

STATION.	Dist. from Charlestown Navy Yard.	Height of river bed above m'n low water of Boston harbor.	Area of section at low water.	Area of section at high water.	Depth at low water of Oct. 3d.	Depth at high water of Oct. 3d.
	Miles.	Feet.	Sq. feet.	Sq. feet.	Feet.	Feet.
Charlestown Dry Dock.....................	0	−24.7	27363	41545	24.8	34.2
Mystic River, 1 mile above Dry Dock	1	− 8.0	8003	24049	8.0	17.4
Boston and Maine R. R. Bridge...........	2½	− 5.2	869	17019	5.3	14.7
Ten Hills.....................................	3	− 5.3	676	4527	5.3	14.6
Medford Bridge.............................	5	− 0.1	19	530	1.2	9.5
Near Herring Weir..........................	6¾	+ 4.3	149	506	1.8	4.6
Near Wood's Mill..........................	7¼	+ 6.6	76	430	0.7	2.8
Weir Bridge	7½	+ 5.1	63	74	3.5	4.0
Narrows of Mystic Pond...................	8	....	70	90	1.7	1.8

NOTE. The areas given above must not be regarded as those of the *moving* sections, which are always less than those of the channel.

TABLE 2.

Table of Hourly Changes of Tides and Currents in Mystic Ponds and River.

Datum line 5.50 feet below mean low water of Boston Harbor.

Time. H.M.	Charlestown Dry Dock. Height.	Vel.	Ten Hills. Height.	Vel.	Medford Bridge. Height.	Vel.	Herring Weir. Height.	Vel.	Below Wood's Mill. Height.	Vel.	Weir Bridge. Height.	Vel.	Lower Mystic I'd at Niles's Boat House. Height.	Vel.	Mystic Pond at Narrows. Heft	Vel.
	Feet.	Miles.	Feet.	Miles.	Feet.	Miles.	Feet.	Miles.	Feet.	Miles.	Feet.	Mlrs.	Feet.	Vel.		Miles.
7.00	5.55 L.W. (5.54 feet) at 7h 11m	+0.30	6.06 L.W. (5.65 feet) at 7h 36m	−0.05	7.03	−1.68	11.64	−1.00	12.83	−1.36	14.17	−0.97	14.53			−0.50
8.00	6.35	+0.40	5.95	+0.05	6.63 L.W. (6.57 feet) at 8h 15m	−1.54	11.64	−1.00	12.83	−1.36	14.15	−0.97	14.52			−0.50
9.00	7.76	+0.30	7.40	+0.30	7.20	−0.38	11.64	−0.90	12.83	−1.36	14.13	−0.57	14.52			−0.50
10.00	9.56	+0.30	9.25	+0.40	8.82	+0.64	11.64	−0.90	12.83	−1.36	14.13	−0.97	14.52			−0.50
11.00	11.41	+0.13	11.20	+0.30	10.96	+1.31	11.64	−0.83	12.83	−1.36	14.13	−0.90	14.51			−0.52
12.00	13.31	+0.30	13.35	+0.30	13.05	+1.17	12.95	+0.30	12.86	−1.20	14.13	−0.90	14.51			−0.62
13.00	14.76 H.W. (14.90 ft.) at 13h 20m	+0.10	14.80 H.W. (14.90 ft.) at 13h 24m	+0.20	14.67	+0.97	14.55	+0.45	14.34	0.00	14.50	0.00	14.51			−0.45
14.00	14.60	−0.20	14.70	−0.05	14.85 H.W. (14.94 ft.) at 13h 30m	0.00	14.89 H.W. at 13h 46m	+0.15	14.92 H.W. at 14h 02m	+0.44	14.72	+1.40	14.60 H.W. at 14h 45m			+0.30
15.00	13.31	−0.35	13.30	−0.20	13.44	−1.17	13.03	−0.60	11.23	−0.39	14.52	0.00	14.63			0.00

Currents too feeble to be accurately measured. (Lower Mystic, Vel.)

TABLE 2. (Continued.)

Datum line 5.50 feet below mean low water of Boston Harbor.

Time.	Charlestown Dry Dock.		Ten Hills.		Medford Bridge.		Herring Weir.		Below Wood's Mill.		Weir Bridge.		Lower Mystic P'd at Niles's Boat House.		Mystic Pond at Narrows.	
H. M.	Height.	Vel.	Height.	Vel.	Height.	Vel.	Height.	Vel.	Height.	Vel.	Height.	Vel.	Height.	Vel.	Hei't.	Vel.
	Feet.	Miles.	Feet.	Miles.	Feet.	Miles.	Feet.	Miles.	Feet.	Miles.	Feet.	Miles.	Feet.	Currents too feeble to be accurately meas.		Miles.
16.00	11.51	−0.45	11.55	−0.45	11.92	−1.30	12.90	−0.83	13.30	−0.83	14.22	−0.91	14.61		……	−0.35
17.00	9.61	−0.53	9.90	−0.55	10.25	−1.72	11.64	−0.97	12.89	−1.30	14.18	−0.97	14.60		……	−0.60
18.00	7.41	−0.70	8.25	−0.60	8.73	−1.96	11.64	−1.00	12.88	−1.40	14.17	−1.05	14.60		……	−0.70
19.00	5.70 L. W. at 19h 37m	−0.65	6.60	−0.60	7.48	−1.94	11.64	−1.00	12.87	*1.40	14.17	−1.05	14.60		……	−0.65
20.00	5.50	0.00	5.55	−0.20	6.73	−1.42	11.64	−1.00	12.87	*1.38	14.16	−1.05	14.60		……	−0.62
Deepest part of chann'l bed.	Feet. 19.2	……	Feet. 0.2	……	Feet. .5.4.	……	Feet. .9.8.	……	Feet. .12.1.	……	Feet. 10.6.	……	Feet. −65.5	……	Feet. 13.	…
Distances from Charlesto'n Dry Dock.		……	Miles. 3	……	Miles. .5.	……	Miles. .6½.	……	Miles. .7½.	……	Miles. .7½.	……	Miles. .7½.	……	Miles. .8.	…

NOTE. The tides of "Dry Dock," "Ten Hills," "Medford Bridge," "Herring Weir," "Wood's Mill," and "Lower Mystic Pond," were simultaneously observed on Oct. 3, 1860; the same is true of the currents of the second, third, and fourth of those stations; the other quantities of the above table have been supplied from corrected observations of other dates.

* Interpolated.

TABLE 3.

Tides and Currents of Mystic Pond and River.

Date	STATION	Tides H. Water (h.m.)	Tides L. Water (h.m.)	Time of day Fl'd to ebb (h.m.)	Time of day Ebb to fl'd (h.m.)	Current turns Aft. loc'l tide Fl'd to ebb (h.m.)	Current turns Aft. loc'l tide Ebb to fl'd (h.m.)	After tide of Ch. D. D'k Tides H. Water (m.)	After tide of Ch. D. D'k Tides L. Water (h.m.)	Currents Fl'd to ebb (h.m.)	Currents Ebb to fl'd (h.m.)	Durations Currents Flood (h.m.)	Durations Currents Ebb (h.m.)	Slack Between fld and ebb (m.)	Slack Between ebb and flood (m.)
1860 Aug. 28.	Dry Dock	9 37	15 42	9 25	16 25	− 0 12				− 0 12	0 43	5 27	7 00	50	5
" 28	Dry Dock	22 00		21 52	4 58		0 43			− 0 08	0 41		7 06	43	15
" 29	Dry Dock	10 27	4 17												
" 29	Dry Dock	22 45	16 35												
" 30	Dry Dock	11 10	5 02												
" 30	Weir Bridge	11 53		22 17	17 20			43			0 45	4 57	7 42	79	24
" 29	Mystic River (1 mile above Dry Dock)	11 50	5 37	10 52	5 59					− 0 28	0 57	4 53		16	8
" 30	Mystic River (1 mile above Dry Duck)	12 30				50				− 0 18					
" 31	Dry Dock	12 30	18 32	13 20	11 34			40	30	1 30	5 57	1 46		01	01
" 31	Weir Bridge	12 38	lost	14 08	12 25					2 18	6 48	1 43	6 45	45	10
" 31	Narrows (Mystic Pond)	12 56	16 45to?												
Sept. 1	Dry Duck	13 25	7 15	12 30	19 15	08		08		0	0 43	5 35?		11	10
" 1	Ten Hills	13 37	7 45	13 15	11 00	19		26		45	4 42	2 15		03	01
" 3	Herring Weir	14 06	7 46	14 30	13 06	24		12	30	65		1 24		15	15
" 3	Dry Dock	14 00	20 12	20 51				41	22						04
" 3	Ten Hills	14 00	8 08					0	59						
" 4	Wood's Mill	14 15	8 46	14 35	9 32	20	47	15		20	47	5 03		06	02
" 4	Dry Dock	2 15	8 21	15 36	13 18	51		45		1 36	5 33	2 18		12	24
" 5	Boston and Maine Railroad Bridge	14 35		2 20 14 51	8 54			10	46	05 16	33	5 29 5 51	6 34	40 88	12
Oct. 3	Medford Bridge	14 45	9 07	13 50	7 45	29		01 17 41	20 1 04	30 *38 1 23	34 2 01 5 56	6 06 4 46 1 36		20 03 03	15 01 04
" 3	Dry Dock	13 21	7 11	13 58	9 12	21	14								
" 3	Ten Hills	13 37	8 15	14 43	13 07	42	57								
" 3	Wood's Mill	14 01													

* Gauge above bridge. — not the same as above referred to

TABLE 4.

General grouping of results from tidal and current observations of Mystic Pond and River.

STATIONS	Distance.	TIDES. Delay of wave. High water.	Low water.	CURRENTS. Delay after D. D'k tide. Turning from flood to ebb.	Turning from ebb to flood.	Durations of Flood.	Ebb.	Sl'k water. At turning from flood to ebb.	At turning from ebb to flood.
	Miles.	h. m.	h. m.	h. m.	h. m.	h. m.	h. m.	h. m.	h. m.
Charlestown Dry Dock........	0	......	......	10	42	5 27	7 03	46	10
Mystic River (1 mile above dry dock).......................	1	......	......	23	51	4 55	7 42	48	16
Boston & Maine R. R. bridge..	2½	......	......	10	33	5 43	6 34	64	08
Ten Hills	3	05	24	15	38	5 50	6 45	16	12
Medford Bridge...............	5	14	52	29	1 24	4 56	......	04	02
Herring Weir..................	6¾	26	......	45	4 42	2 15	......	03	01
Wood's Mill..................	7¼	42	......	1 20	5 44	1 46	......	10.	15
Weir Bridge	7½	42*	......	1 30	5 57	1 46	......	01	01
Narrows	8	......	......	2 18	6 48	1 43	......	45	10

* Result from a single comparison.

TABLE 5.

Temperatures and Specific Gravities of Mystic Ponds.

	LOWER POND.						UPPER POND.				
Date, 1860.	Time.	Depth.	Period of Immersion.	Temperature.	State of water.	Date, 1860.	Time.	Depth.	Period of Immersion.	Temperature.	State of water.
Sept. 1.	h. m. 14 15	feet. 1	m.	74°	Fresh.	Sept. 1.	h. m. 18 15	feet. 1	m. 10	73°	Fresh.
	15 10	10	10	73	"		18 25	10	10	73½	"
	15 00	20	10	66	Sulphur's and salt.		18 35	20	10	71	"
	14 50	40	10	59	"		18 45	40	10	62½	"
	14 40	75	10	58	"		....	.....	.....	...	....

TABLE 6.

LOWER POND (Above the Shoal).						UPPER POND.					
Date. 1860.	Time.	Depth.	Period of Immersion.	Temperature.	Specific Gravity	State of Water.	Date. 1860.	Time.	Depth.	Temperature.	Specific Gravity.	State of Water.
	h. m.	ft.	'm.					h. m.	ft.			
Sept. 10	15 05	1		64°	1.0004	Fresh.	Sept. 10	17 45	1	70°	0.9996	Fresh.
	15 25	18	10	64°	1.0031	Salt.		17 11	70	57°	1.0004	Fresh.
	16 12	22	8	60°	1.0055	Sulphurous and Salt.						
	16 30	50	8	61°	1.0081							

10

TABLE 7.

Winter Temperatures of Mystic Ponds, Jan. 2, 1861.

LOWER POND.				UPPER POND.			
Time.	Depth.	Temp.	Remarks.	Time.	Depth.	Temp.	Remarks.
h. m.	feet.			h. m.	feet.		
12	1	33°	A bleached cotton line, saturated with acetate of lead, detected sulphurous mat-ter at 21-22 feet depth. The height of the water at Niles's boat house was 15 feet.	14.42	1	82½°	
	2	33½			....	....	
	10	33½			10	34½	
	18	38½			....	....	
	19	33			....	....	
	19½	39½			....	....	
	21	42¾			....	....	
	24	42			80	36	
	40	42½			....	....	
	50	43			50	37½	
14	04	45		15.30	60	36½	First trial.
					60	37½	Second trial.

For the above observations the period of immersion for the thermometer was, in each case, seven minutes.

At Weir Bridge, the stream flowing into the ponds (15h. 50m.) was found to be quite free from ice, with a temperature of 34°. The water was fresh.

HENRY MITCHELL, Asst. C. S., Observer.

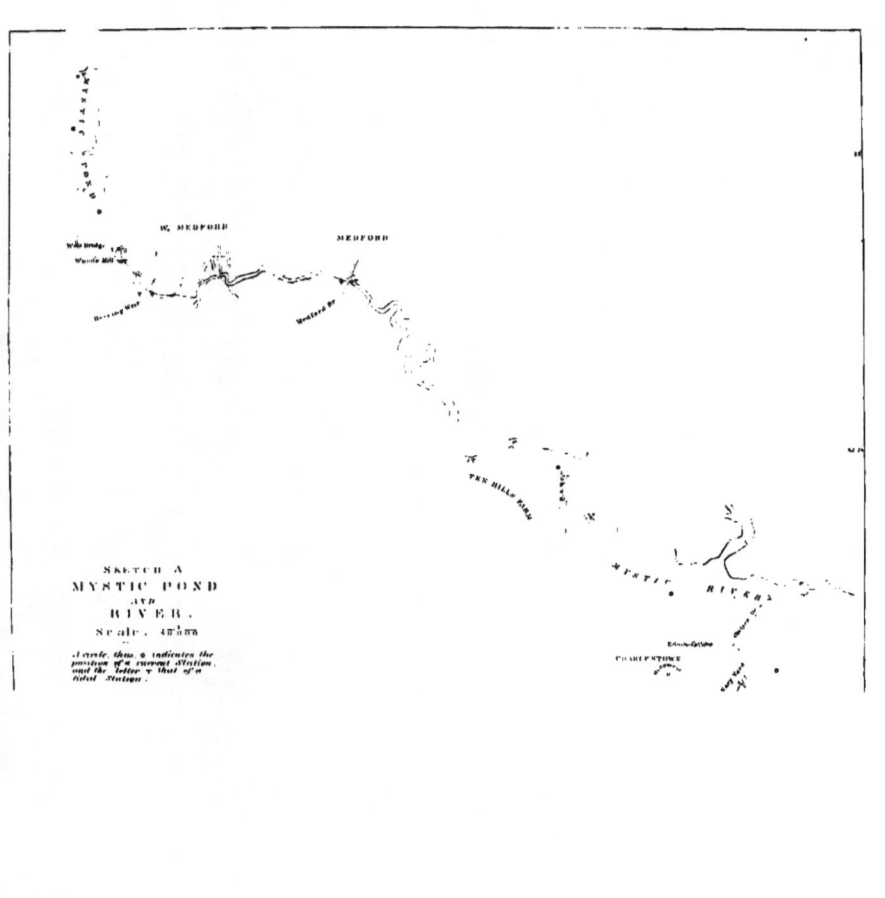

SKETCH A
MYSTIC POND
AND
RIVER.
Scale. 40000

A circle, thus, ○ indicates the
position of a current Station,
and the letter τ that of a
tidal Station.

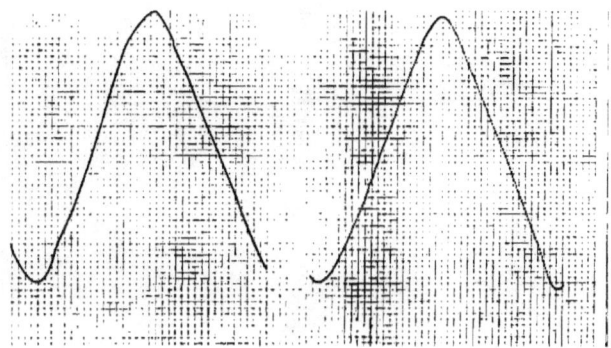

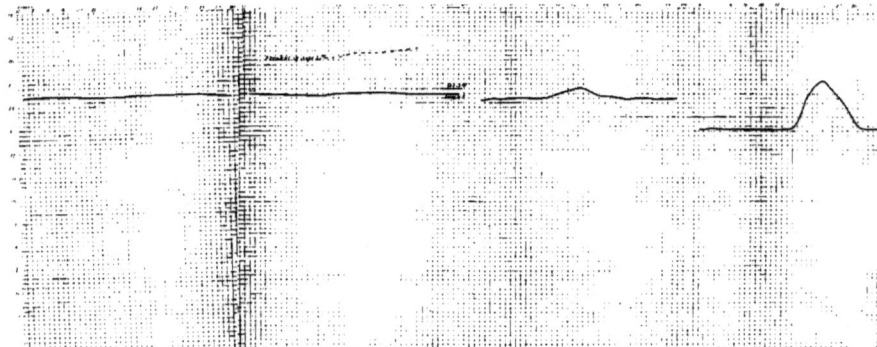

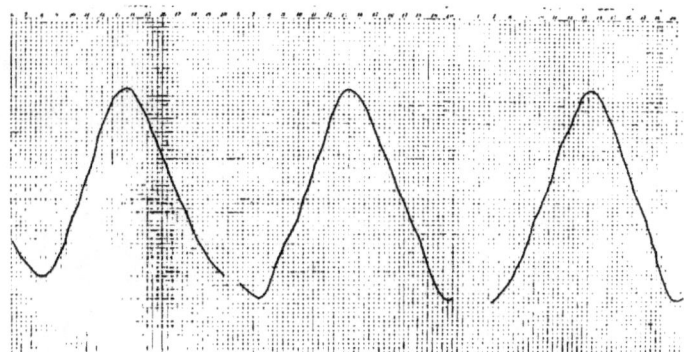

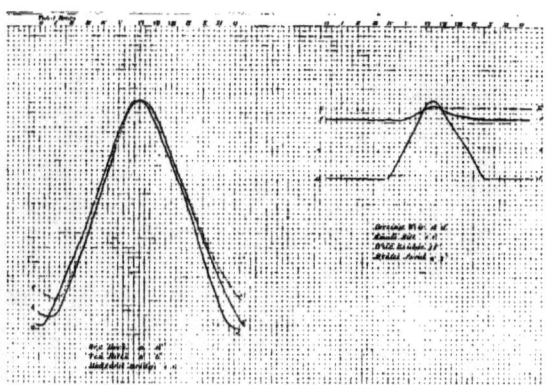

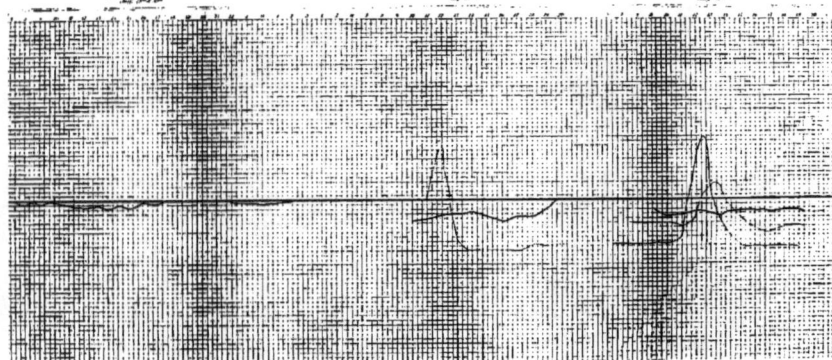

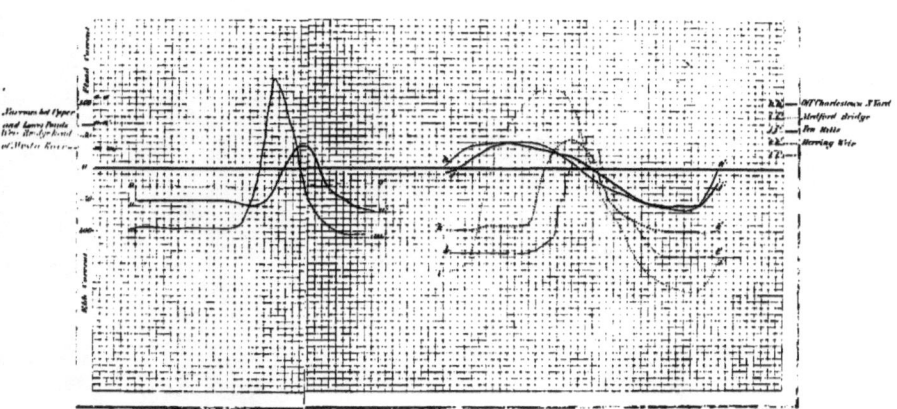

D₁

DURATIONS
OF
FLOOD CURRENTS

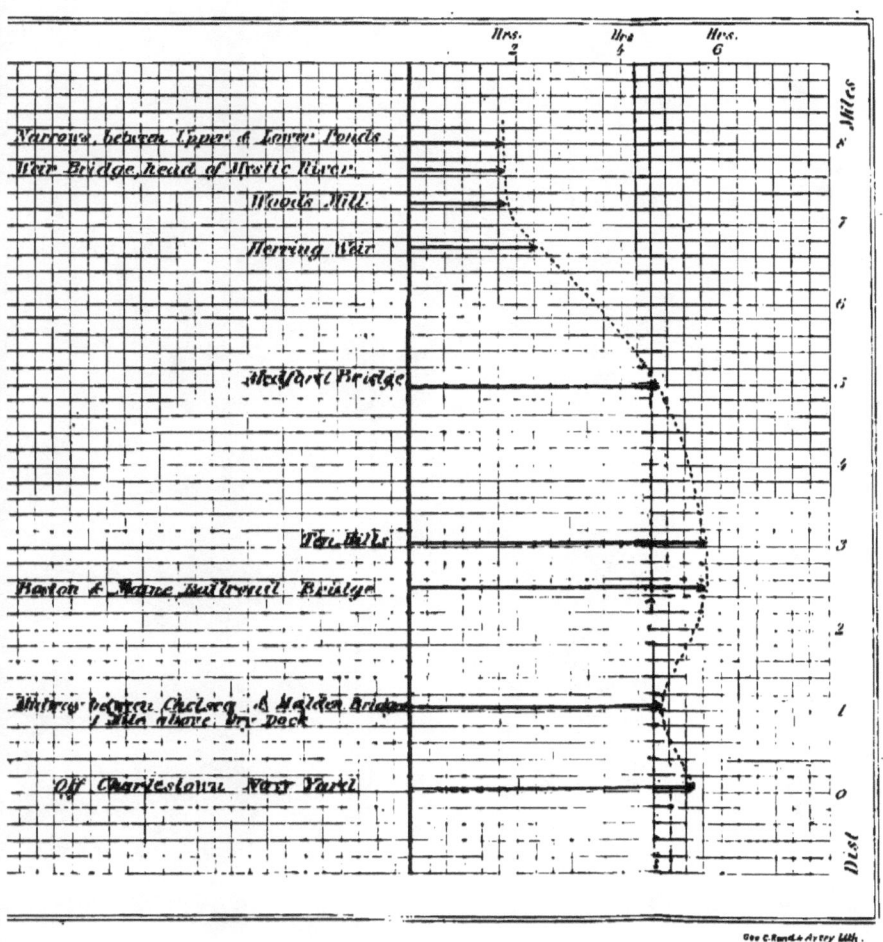

DURATIONS
OF
SLACK WATER.

F
WINTER TEMPERATURES.
Obs'ns. of Jan. 2d 1861

Lower Mystic Pond   Upper Mystic Pond

Geo C. Rand & Avery lith.

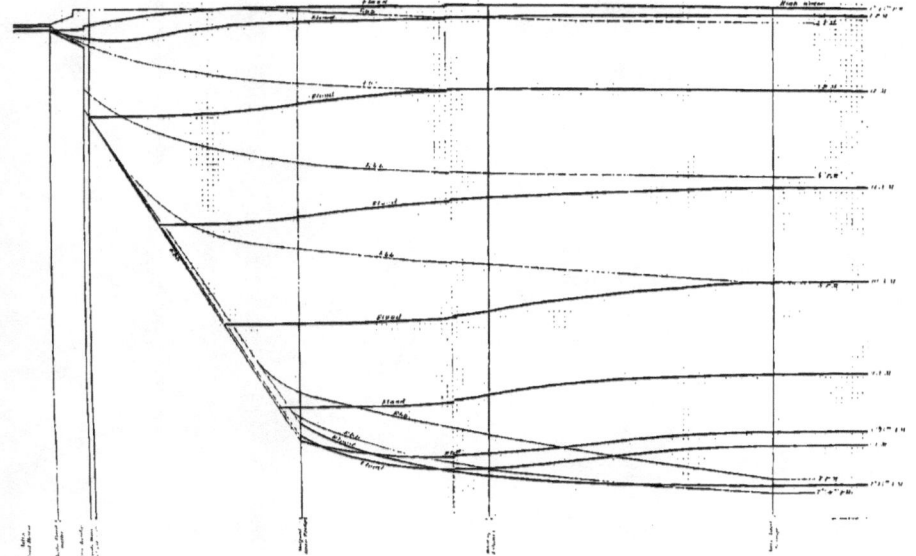

APPENDIX.

MR. STEVENSON'S LETTER.

ENGINEER'S OFFICE, BUNKER HILL BANK BUILDING, }
CHARLESTOWN, MASS., NOV. 22, 1860. }

DEAR SIR: My absence at New York has prevented me from earlier complying with your request to place in writing the substance of my remarks, made to you a few days since, relative to Mystic Pond and River, explaining that the proposed constructions of the City of Charlestown to enable them to obtain a supply of pure water from this pond, in place of being detrimental to Mystic River and the Harbor of Boston, would rather be made to subserve the interests of both; or, in other words, that, by artificial erections controlling the flow into and from Mystic Pond, an amount of fresh water may be diverted for the use of the city, while the quantity of water of value as a scouring agent of the river is not diminished, but such agent can be made of greater value than at present.

From the facts adduced in recent careful and extended investigations made under the direction of your Commision, by Mr. Henry Mitchell, and with whom I had the pleasure of co-operating, we ascertain —

First, that Wood's Mill is about the limit of the tidal wave of the ocean in Mystic River.

Second, that Mystic Pond is not a tidal reservoir of present value to Boston Harbor.

Third, that owing to the elevation of the bed of Mystic River, north and west of Medford Bridge, above low-water mark of Boston Harbor, the fresh water from Mystic Pond continues to run ebb from five to six hours after the commencement of flood at the harbor; and the colliding of these currents, by checking the velocity of the flow, is detrimental to the tidal action on the bed of the river.

Your intimate knowledge of the details of the recent investigations renders unnecessary, on my part, much explanation of the reasons which lead us to the foregoing conclusions. The peculiar condition of

Mystic Lower Pond proves unequivocally the occasional admixture of sea water, but an examination of all the data presented shows that the limit of the wave up the river is at Wood's Mill. The average volume of the flood current into Mystic Pond, as found from observations, is one million cubic feet, or seven and a half million gallons, at every tide. Had the observations been continued for a longer period, or for a year, so as to bring into the account the neap tides, and the seasons when the height of the pond is such that no current can pass into it from the river, this average would doubtless be much less. While the volume of the flow into the pond is possibly of some little value to the *river*, the proportion which it bears to the average tidal inflow above Chelsea Bridge, less than $\frac{1}{310}$, is too small to allow of its effects being appreciable in the *harbor*, even were the pond not at so great a distance from the latter that its waters do not in one tide reach it.

The average duration of the ebb at Mystic Pond is 20 hours a day (or 10 hours for each tide), during which time the daily fresh-water yield, and the water flowed into the pond from the river, must pass out of the pond.

Now we find that of the ten hours of ebb, there are but about five hours during which the ebb current is unobstructed, the flood current colliding therewith during the remaining five hours. *The volume of water, then, which flows down during the first five hours of the ebb, is alone of value in acting as a scouring agent,* and that only in the upper reaches of the river.

It should be borne in mind that the time taken in passing from Wood's Mill to head of estuary, 4¼ miles, is 3¾ hours, as calculated from observations. Hence, there remains but 1¼ hours during which *water from Mystic Pond* passes below the head of the estuary. To reach Chelsea Bridge, 2¼ miles further, assuming the maximum velocity observed at any time of ebb tide of October 3,—viz: six tenths of a mile per hour,—requires four hours ten minutes; or, in other words, *the tide would have turned to run flood at Chelsea Bridge some three hours before a drop of water from Mystic Pond could have reached Chelsea Bridge.*

Hence the conclusion that, as a tidal reservoir, Mystic Pond is not of present value to Boston Harbor.

As an exemplification of the colliding of the ebb and flood currents, let us take the tidal observations of October 3 (*vide* annexed plot of same). On this day the flood current commenced at the Navy Yard at 7^h 15^m A. M., while it continued to run ebb at Wood's Mill until 1^h 9^m P. M., a period of 5^h 54^m.

An average of observations made on board the schooner Bailey, and at the current stations, numbered 4, 6, and 7, at other dates than October 3, shows the duration of stand at flood at various points, as follows : —

Broad Sound — 7^m.

Tidal Station. No. 9 — Mystic River above Chelsea Bridge, 43^m ; the day-tide stand being 58^m, the night, 28^m.

T. S. No. 8 — Above B. & M. R. R., 51^m ; the day-tide stand being 1^h 23^m ; the night, 40^m.

T. S. No. 7 — Head of Estuary above Ten Hills Farm, 19^m.

T. S. Nos. 6 and 4 — Medford Bridge and Wood's Mill, 9^m each.

If the fresh waters flowing from Mystic Pond be retained in the pond during such hours as recent investigations indicate that the tidal inflow up the river would be thereby increased by an amount nearly equal to the volume of the fresh-water yield, or as much less as may be found most advisable, a sufficient amount of water for Charlestown or Chelsea may be diverted, and the balance of retained fresh water thrown in in aid of the increased tidal waters at such time of the ebb as experience and investigation show it to be of most benefit to the river. This will admit of as complete, if not better and surer, scouring action than at present.

In the making a tidal reservoir of that space now occupied by the fresh-water flow from the pond, may we not so far imitate nature in the action observable in tidal reservoirs as to expect like results ? Let us suppose Mystic Pond raised as proposed for the "high level" (*vide* Water Report, Baldwin & Stevenson), six feet higher than at present, with a dam at its outlet near Weir Bridge, so as to make it a fresh-water reservoir. The average fresh-water yield of the pond in 1859 was estimated at 23¼ million gallons per day ; when acting as a storage reservoir, we may safely assume the available yield at all times to equal twenty million gallons, or ten million for each tide. The maximum amount of water required for Charlestown and Chelsea, estimating for 100,000 persons, is six million gallons per day, or three million for twelve hours ; this leaves some seven million gallons, with six feet head available *to increase the tidal flow down the river at every ebb.* If we suppose the flow from Mystic Pond stopped so that none of the water flowing therefrom remains in the bed of the river above the estuary at the commencement of flood at that point, the tidal flow up the river will be increased by an amount equal to the retained fresh water; or taking a similar tide to that of October 3 .as an example, some nine million gallons more of tidal water would have passed into the river at each tide.   Having some seven million gallons of water in addition to this, under control, with a head of six feet, it would seem that the proposed erections, so far from being detrimental, would enable us much more completely to conserve the channel, *as far, at least, as the head of the estuary*, as the loss now due to the meeting of the flood and ebb currents is avoided, while we have it in our power to increase the velocity of the ebb, and the quantity of water that is of value, if at any time desirable.

Very truly yours,

C. L. STEVENSON.

CAPT. C. H. DAVIS, *Cambridge*.

PROF. HORSFORD'S REPORT.

GEN. J. G. TOTTEN, *Pres. Boston Harbor Commission :* —

In reply to the inquiries submitted to me in Mr. Mitchell's letter of 9th of September last, I beg to submit the following Report : —

The inquiries were —

1. " The amount of saline and mineral matter in general as compared with standard pure water ? "

2. " If an excess of certain ingredients is found, whence their source,—local, or from influx of the sea ? "

3. " If from the sea, do the conditions indicate frequent or rare renewals of sea water ? "

4. " Are the muds strongly impregnated with mineral salts or other substances, calculated to contaminate spring water long in contact with them ? "

The communication of Mr. Mitchell was accompanied by a number of samples of water from the surface, and from various depths of the upper and lower Mystic Ponds, from Mystic River, and from different depths of Spy and Fresh Ponds. There was also submitted a suite of muds from the bottoms of these ponds, and from the mud flats and other points of the Mystic River, to which, and also to the supply of waters, additions were frequently made by Mr. Mitchell and Mr. Stevenson. There were also supplied samples of copper wire rope, and strips of silver-plated copper, that had been suspended in vertical position for various lengths of time in the above waters, to ascertain their action on these metals.

The accompanying schedules exhibit the results of the analytical examination of the above samples.

Schedule A gives the specific gravities and the relative amounts of saline and organic matters in 1,000 cubic centimetres of each of the several waters, together with the temperatures and depths of the waters as far as observed at the time they were taken, and the temperatures at which the specific gravities were determined.

Schedule B gives the taste, color, and sediments of the various waters.

Schedule C gives the relative amounts of inorganic and organic matters in the various muds, dried at a temperature of 212° F.

Schedule D gives the results of the examination of the waters and muds of different localities, in regard to the origin of the peculiar sulphurous taste and smell found in the deep water of the Lower Mystic Pond.

Schedule E gives the residue of samples of water from the Lower Mystic Pond, in vertical lines taken from holes through the ice, furnishing the data for the curves F. and G.

To enable me the more fully to comprehend the inquiries, I have twice visited the Pond, and examined the outlet on Mystic River as far as Charlestown, besides making an expedition to Fresh and Spy Ponds.

.

COMPARISON OF THE MYSTIC POND WATER WITH STANDARD PURE WATER.

The water which stands first in relative purity in the neighborhood of Boston is that of Lake Cochituate, from which Boston derives its supplies. Compared with this, Fresh Pond and Spy Pond waters, which are eminently soft and well suited to domestic use, have more than twice the amount of foreign matter. The Upper Mystic Pond water has nearly twice the measure of foreign matter that either Spy Pond or Fresh Pond water has, — and the surface of the Lower Mystic has nearly twice and a half times as much as the surface of the Upper Mystic. At a point above the bar, the amount is more than five times as great. From the surface down, the measure of mineral and vegetable matters increases until the amount is nearly twelve times as great as that at the surface.

Cochituate contains				0.0534 in 1000 parts.
Fresh Pond	"	28 feet from surface,	0.1076 " " "
Spy Pond	"	25 " " "	0.1056 " " "
Upper Mystic	"	surface,	0.2026 " " "
Lower Mystic	"	"	0.4804 " " "
"	"	" upon bar,	1.0354
"	"	18 feet from surface,	6.4996
"	"	22 " " "	9.4558
"	"	40 " " "	12.6806
"	"	70 " " "	13.6120

Notwithstanding this considerable increase over the Cochituate, and Fresh, and Spy Pond waters, on comparison with the following standard waters, the result will be seen to be not unfavorable.

Croton water contains, in 1,000 parts,   0.4350
Fairmount   "   "   "   "   0.6014

The relative amounts of inorganic and organic matters are perhaps not quite so favorable, as the following table will show.

					Inorganic Residue.	Organic Residue.
Cochituate	-	-	-	-	77.16	22.84
Fresh Pond	-	-	-	-	66.92	33.08
Spy Pond	-	-	-	-	65.35	34.65
Croton	-	-	-	-	31.21	68.79
Fairmount	-	-	-	-	65.69	34.31
Upper Mystic (surface)		-	-		71.28	28.72
Lower Mystic (")		-	-		75.69	24.31
" " (" above bar)					77.60	22.40

There is not, however, an amount of mineral matter that would deprive the surface water of the qualities of sweetness and softness. This is true of the Upper Pond, and of the surface of the Lower Pond. From the surface down, the total and relative amounts of mineral matter increase, and as two of the constituents of the water, the salt of lime and the salt of magnesia, decompose soluble soaps, forming insoluble lime and magnesia soaps, the water at moderate depths is unsuitable for the laundry.

The accompanying curve F exhibits the increase in saline matters from the surface down; and the curve G the total amount of residue, inorganic and organic. K exhibits the saline matter in the Upper Pond. The curve I, plotted from Mr. Mitchell's observations, given in Table 7 of the Report of the Boston Harbor Commission, exhibits the relations of the winter temperatures (they were made January 2, 1861) to the amount of saline matter at the different depths. The curve J, from the same source, enforces the illustration by exhibiting the temperatures at various depths of the Upper Pond at the same date.

The water of the Lower Pond, twenty feet from the surface, possesses, in addition to a brackish taste, a sulphurous smell and taste, and these peculiarities become more and more offensive at greater depths down to the bottom. At depths above forty feet, the water which is quite transparent when drawn, after standing a few days, parts with the offensive smell and taste, but without losing, in any degree, its transparency. At a depth of seventy feet, water also clear when drawn, after a few days' exposure to the air, loses its highly offensive sulphurous smell and taste, and at the same time becomes cloudy from the separation of sulphur. The upper limit of this sulphurous stratum in two localities especially observed, was very precisely nineteen feet and nine inches from the surface. At this point it is little more than perceptible, but increases in intensity of offensiveness downward, as the above statement in regard to the separation of sulphur shows. It was noted to be at about twenty feet in several other localities. At eighteen feet, the offensive smell and taste were not perceptible. At twenty-five feet, although the smell was perceptible on the day of collection, it was not recognizable two days after, nor could a reaction for a volatile sulphurous compound be obtained; while from a depth of sixty-two feet, it was readily perceptible to the senses for several days, and gave a prompt and decided chemical reaction.

The sulphurous body, which, at first thought, one would conceive to be either hydro-sulphuric acid or a volatile sulphide, as of ammonium, failed to give any precipitate, either with acetate of lead or perchloride of mercury, which, in the presence of abundant chlorides, is a better reagent. But on boiling the water with a mineral acid, and collecting the distillate, it gave a prompt black precipitate with sugar of lead, — a proof that there was present a complex compound which the mineral acid and heat decomposed, producing hydro-sulphuric acid.

The curve H exhibits the relative amounts of sulphide of lead formed from equal volumes of water at the depths indicated, the quantity becoming inappreciable at a little more than twenty feet from the surface.

This sulphurous body readily acts on metals. A copper wire rope, vertically suspended, became, in the course of twelve hours, thickly coated with sulphide of copper up to within nineteen feet nine inches of the surface; and a strip of copper plated with silver on one side became coated from the same limit downward on the copper side, with brown sulphide, but the silver, except in two points indicated in the columns L and M, was left quite untarnished.

This capacity of the Lower Mystic Pond water to act on bright metal surfaces, is possessed to a less extent by Fresh and Spy Pond waters. Silver-copper strips were lowered in both these Ponds, two in each. The detailed results are given in Schedule D. In Fresh Pond, at a depth of twenty-nine and one half feet from the surface, the action on copper and silver is observable in four and a half hours. In twelve hours, it extends through a depth of seven feet, where the sulphide formed is deepest, and for two feet farther, where the action is less marked. Beyond this point, the silver and copper remain bright to within one foot of the bottom.

In Spy Pond, the action commences at a point about twenty feet from the surface, and in twelve hours the silver and copper were deeply tarnished through the next eight feet two inches, less so through the following two feet, and for the last two feet the metals remained bright in one locality. In another locality, the metals were bright for one foot three inches only from the bottom upward. It is a peculiarity not so readily explained, that both the silver and copper are here tarnished, while in the Lower Mystic it was the copper chiefly.

It is quite apparent, upon an inspection of the samples of exposed metals, that the corroding agent is much less vigorous in Fresh and Spy Ponds than in the Lower Mystic. In the deeper parts of Cochituate Lake, no such stratum of sulphurous water has been observed. The consideration of the conditions in which these ponds differ from each other, leads to the second inquiry, to wit: —

"*If an excess of certain ingredients is found, whence their source, — local, or from influx of the sea ?*"

A detailed analysis of the water taken from the bottom of the Lower Mystic, made by Dr. Hayes and published in the recent Report of Messrs. Baldwin and Stevenson, gives the constituents of sea water in about the proportions in which they occur in the open sea. The amount of saline matter is, compared with sea water, only about as 1 to 2.56,— that is, it is of the constitution of sea water diluted with nearly *one* and *a half* times its volume of pure water.

The water of Cochituate Lake contains in general the same constituents that are found in Fresh Pond, Spy Pond, and the tributaries to the Upper Mystic. The waters of the last three, although containing each a larger percentage of mineral matter than the Cochituate, are, as already intimated, eminently pure.

It is only in the deeper water of the Lower Mystic that the excess of certain ingredients is found, to wit, of the constituents which, sufficiently concentrated, constitute sea water, and of a peculiar sulphurous compound which is quite a new feature in the ponds of a region of primitive geology.

Is the salt water due to springs? The fact that the water of the Upper Mystic lying in the same primitive basin is free from all excess of saline matter is against this supposition.

Two other modes of derivation have been suggested for the salt water, one by percolation through the soil from the Mystic River, and the other by inflow of salt water at high tide.

If the former were true, the neighboring wells in which the waters do not stand above the level of the tide, would be likely to be more or less impregnated with salt; but of this there has been no complaint.

It is moreover well known, that, on the point of Cape Cod, and in other similar localities, the wells sunk quite near the shore, in which the water rises and falls strictly with the tide, do not partake of the brackish character of sea water.

That percolation does not take place at the greater depths, may be inferred from the fact that it does not take place near the surface. The mud near the outlet,— at a depth of eight feet,— and which, if the sea water came through the soil bearing its offensive smell and taste, would contain sulphurous matters, was found to be entirely free from them.

There is against this mode of supply the well-known fact that in under drainage, where the tiles are but two or three feet below the surface, however much manure may have been spread on the soil above, the water that escapes is quite pure. In addition to all these considerations, there is the fact of the fully adequate agency in the supply of sea water at extreme high tide. On such occasions the sea water entering the pond through the outlet, by virtue of its greater specific gravity flows along the bed of the pond and takes its position at the bottom.

Here, by the law of diffusion, the salt water is diluted by rising into the purer water above.

Is the sulphurous compound due to sulphur springs at the bottom of the Pond? To answer this question, let us consider the source of the hydro-sulphuric acid of sulphur springs generally.

In the Pyrenees, where the sulphur springs have been more carefully investigated than perhaps those of any other region, the opinion entertained by chemists is that the sulphur is present as a sulphide of sodium, accompanied by a small amount of free hydro-sulphuric acid.

The source of this sulphide is doubtless to be found in reducing agencies, such as organic matter, acting on sulphates. The familiar case of the formation of iron pyrites in the body of a rat that fell into a solution of sulphate of iron, is in point. The observation by Bastick, that a spring water, containing gypsum in solution, on being agitated with a little ethereal oil, closely stoppered and set aside for three months, became saturated with hydro-sulphuric acid, while the ethereal oil disappeared, is a further illustration of the same point. Now in such a primitive region sulphates and organic matters, if not wanting in the rocks, are at least as likely to supply the upper as they are the lower pond with sulphurous compounds. And as the Upper Pond is absolutely wanting in sulphurous water at any depth, it is rendered eminently improbable that the sulphurous matters of the deeper parts of the lower pond are derived from the earth and rock below. There are, however, two considerations which are quite conclusive. All strictly sulphurous spring water is instantaneously blackened on the addition of acetate of lead, while the water from the bottom of the Lower Mystic is not blackened by this reagent. This experiment shows, as did the test with perchloride of mercury, that there is neither hydro-sulphuric acid nor sulphide of any alkaline base or earth present in the water. It is only on boiling the water with mineral acid, as already remarked, and testing the distillate, that proof of the presence of a sulphur compound is obtained. The second consideration is this,—that when the sediment at the bottom of the pond, where the offensive taste and smell prevail, is examined, the surface sediment is found to contain the sulphurous compound, while that from a depth of a few inches contains little or none of it.

This source set aside, there remains a probable one in the agency to which the excess of saline matters is ascribed, to wit, the sea water.

Now whether the total offensive smell and taste go in with the sea water, or a part only, or none of it; or whether the source of the offensive smell and taste is in the mud at the bottom of the Lower Pond, — it being assumed that the mud has been brought in by sea water, — are questions that have been severally raised and submitted to research.

The muds have been subjected to chemical and microscopic examination.

After leaching the mud of both the Upper and Lower Ponds with a view to washing out any and all soluble matters present, the residues were examined for any and all sulphur compounds. The invariable result was a negative one. There were none present.

Now, on the theory that the mud contained bodies which by slow chemical action was evolving soluble sulphurous compounds, after washing out any such compounds ready formed, the residue must contain the parent source from which the soluble bodies were produced. Finding no sulphur, was conclusive that all the sulphur at the bottom of the pond was already in solution, and a constituent of the sea water.

The muds from Medford Bridge, and from the mud flats above the Eastern Railroad Bridge, were found to contain the same sulphur body, chemically speaking, that was found in water from the bottom of the Lower Mystic Pond. That is, they yielded to water the taste and smell of the offensive water from the bottom of the pond, and the substance was not precipitated with acetate of lead.

Moreover, on distilling with sulphuric acid, the hydro-sulphuric acid reaction was instantly obtained from the distillate.

The relative amounts of organic and inorganic matter in the muds of the different localities, showed that the mud at Medford Bridge, and on the flats of Mystic River above the Eastern Railroad Bridge, contained a vastly greater proportion of inorganic matter— such as sand — than the muds from the bottom of the deeper parts of the Lower and Upper Mystic. In the shallow parts of the pond, as near Niles's Boat House, and out of the main current flowing through the pond, the proportion of sand is greater. Where vertical tubes were lowered into the mud in the deeper parts, that from the bottom of the tube, as might have been expected, contained uniformly a less proportion of organic matter. Near the outlet, where the tide and current of the pond met and the suspended matters naturally fell, the amount of organic matter was found to be greater than at any other point observed.

The microscopic examination of the muds, for which I am indebted to Mr. Moore, of the Scientific School, shows the mud from the deeper parts of the Lower Mystic Pond to contain the various forms of naviculæ, and other silicious shields and remains of infusoriæ, that abound in all the fresh waters in the neighborhood of Boston, besides what seemed to be granules from vegetable cells. Those of the Lower Mystic proved to be quite identical with those of the Upper Mystic Pond, except that the Upper contained a greater proportion of granules from vegetable cells. The surface and sub-sediments were much alike in both cases.

In the mud near the outlet of the Lower Mystic Pond there were numberless vegetable cells, and occasional living animalculæ. These had not been observed in the muds from the great depths of the Upper and Lower Ponds.

The mud, from twenty feet above Medford Bridge, contained not more than one fifth as many organic forms as the deeper pond mud. They are much less perfectly preserved, and the variety is much less.

The mud from the flats, above the Eastern Railroad Bridge, did not contain one thirtieth as many organic remains as the mud from the deeper parts of the Lower or Upper Pond; and the sub-sediment contained less than the surface mud. These organic remains were moreover very imperfectly preserved.

Fresh and Spy Pond muds differed from that of the Mystic in that the variety of forms, and the proportion of vegetable cells were greater. There were, besides, some distinct green plants; and all were very perfectly preserved.

As the mud of the Mystic River, just above the Medford Bridge and that from the flats above the Eastern Railroad Bridge, contain, relatively, very few organic remains, and these fragmentary, while the mud at the bottom of the deeper parts of the Lower Mystic abounds in organic remains, distinguished for the perfection of their forms, it

2

is quite obvious that the mud of the latter locality is not derived from the two former.

It is further obvious, from the circumstance that the mud of the Upper Pond, which the tide water does not reach, contains the same remains in nearly the same relative proportions of ingredients that the Lower Pond does, that there is an adequate source of the mud in the pond itself.

As the mud of the neighborhood of Medford Bridge and the flats below, when agitated with water, yields an odor and taste identical to the senses and chemical tests with that of the offensive water of the Lower Mystic, it is obvious that whenever the water, that has flowed over and leached these muds, is by high tide carried into Mystic Pond, the substance of offensive taste and smell must go with it, and in time take its position in the deeper parts of the pond. The ultimate source of this sulphurous body in the mud is, in part, simply decaying organisms, — exuviæ, excrementitious matters, etc., and in part, doubtless, sulphates of sea water acted upon and reduced by the organic matters of the mud.

As the offensive body is not a sulphide of any alkali or alkaline earthy metal which sea water contains, or of ammonium, it might be doubted whether the simple reaction of the sulphates of sea water in the deeper Mystic Pond waters contributes in any considerable degree to its production.

It is conceivable, nevertheless, that the organic matters at the bottom of the pond in contact with the quiescent salt water should, as they decay, more or less reduce the sulphates, and yield sulphurous products which, by some transformation with organic matters, assume the peculiar chemical properties of the offensive body that have been observed ; so that a process analogous to that which takes place in the mud on the flats may be regarded as going forward at the bottom of the Lower Pond.

The advance portion of the tidal current, as high water approaches, steadily leaching the mud of the banks of the Mystic River, and accumulating the offensive extract till it reaches the pond, glides in along the bed, and by virtue of its specific gravity takes its position at the bottom. To these two sources the offensive matter must be ascribed ; and not to the mud at the bottom of the Lower Mystic, or the soil below, or rock, as a source of sulphurous matters.

If we ascribe to a like origin the sulphurous matter in Fresh and

Spy Ponds as evidenced by the action on copper and silver, we have the amount of offensive matter in these ponds bearing something like the same relation to that in the Lower Mystic, which the facilities for the approach of tide water and the measure of offensive mud over which it flows, in the several cases, bear to each other.

There would seem to be spring water free from sulphurous matter coming up in Fresh and Spy Ponds, — keeping the lower portion of the metallic strips bright. But in the Lower Mystic there is no evidence of the existence of such springs.

The offensive body in the Lower Mystic, diluting with the purer water above, as it approaches the surface comes in contact with the oxygen in solution from the air, and is oxidized and destroyed.

Appearances indicate that the occasional supply of salt water, and the influx of fresh water from the Upper Pond and lateral tributaries, are about in equilibrio. With a chart of the pond, and sections of its depths, taken in connection with the chemical determinations already made, and a few additional determinations of the salt water that reaches the pond at high tide, it would not be difficult to ascertain the amount of salt water of a given strength now present in the pond.

The determination of the time required in which to supply this measure of saline matter would necessarily invite some hydrographic observations.

The last inquiry of the series, —" *Are the muds strongly impregnated with mineral salts or other substances calculated to contaminate spring water long in contact with them?* " has been answered incidentally in the discussion of the other points that have been raised.

SUMMARY.

The Upper Mystic Pond is, throughout its depth, an eminently pure and soft water.

The Lower Mystic Pond water is sufficiently pure at the surface, and for a depth of some fifteen feet, to serve the purposes of domestic use.

Beyond the depth of eighteen feet the amount of saline matter is such as to impair the taste, and below twenty feet the presence of sulphurous compounds, offensive to the taste and smell, with increasing saline matter, renders it wholly unfit for use.

The excess of saline matter is due to the inflow, not infiltration, of sea water on the occasions of high tide ; how frequently, and in what quantity, hydrographic observations only can determine. The foregoing observations are quite in keeping with occasional and rare, rather than frequent, supplies of sea water.

The sulphurous body at depths below twenty feet is not due to the decomposition of any mineral constituents in the earth or rock at the bottom or on the sides of the pond. It is not due to the mud at the bottom of the pond spontaneously decomposing in a pure fresh water.

It is conceived, in part, to be extracted from the muds of Mystic River banks and flats, as the incoming tide flows over them and discharges into the pond ; and in part, to the reducing action of the organic matter at the bottom of the pond on the sulphates of the sea water, with which these organic matters of the mud are saturated.

The sea water flowing in at high tide, by virtue of its superior specific gravity, flows to the lower depths of the pond, displacing the purer, lighter water. The saline water, from the bottom up, diminishes but little in density till a level of forty feet from the surface is attained ; from this point up, for fifteen to twenty feet, the diffusion is nearly in inverse ratio to the depth, and for the last twenty feet the density lessens but little to the surface.

If the sea water were shut out, the law of diffusion would obviously require that, in time, all the excess of saline matter should be removed. The action of the inflowing current from the Upper Pond would facilitate this purification.

In closing this Report, I have great pleasure in referring to the care and accuracy with which the numerous determinations, made by my assistant, Mr. Charles Merrick, have been conducted.

Respectfully submitted,

E. N. HORSFORD, *Chemist.*

CAMBRIDGE, Nov. 5, 1860.

A

	Date.	Depth.	Temperature.	Specific Gravity.	At temperature.	C'bic centimetres taken.	Total residue.	Loss at red heat.	Per ct. of inorganic matter.	Per cent. organic matter.
Fresh Pond	Sept. 19,	Feet 28	57°	1.00006	56°	1,000	0.1076	0.0356	66.92	33.08
Fresh Pond	Sept. 19,	40	53°	1.0001	53°.5	1,000	0.1126	0.0428	61.99	38.01
Spy Pond	Sept. 21,	25	64°	1.000	56°	1,000	0.1056	0.0366	65.35	34.65
Spy Pond	......	35	63°	1.0002	54°.5	1,000	0.1148	0.0468	59.24	40.76
Mystic Upper Pond	Sept. 10,	Surface.	......	1.00004	52°	1,000	......	......	......	......
Mystic Upper Pond	......	Surface.	......	......	......	1,000	0.2026	0.0582	71.28	28.72
Mystic Upper Pond	Sept. 10,	70	......	1.0005	50°.25	1,000	0.4748	0.1064	77.60	22.40
Mystic Lower Pond	Sept. 10,	Surface.	......	......	......	1,000	0.4804	0.1165	75.69	24.31
Mystic Lower Pond	......	Surface. Another point	......	1.00001	53°.5	......	......	......	......	......
Mystic Lower Pond	Sept. 10,	Surface. Above bar.	......	1.0008	53°.5	1,000	1.0354	0.2330	77.60	22.40
Mystic Lower Pond	......	18	......	1.0035	52°	1,000	6.4996	2.4900	61.91	38.09
Mystic Lower Pond, above bar	......	22	......	1.0061	50°.25	1,000	9.4558	2.1920	76.82	23.18
Mystic Lower Pond	Aug. 29,	40	......	1.0084	52°	1,000	12.6806	1.8794	65.18	14.82
Mystic Lower Pond	......	70	......	1.0162	53°.5	1,000	13.6120	2.2672	83.35	16.65
Mystic River at Medford Bridge after high water	Oct. 3,	One foot from bottom.	......	1.0002	52°	1,000	0.3040	0.0682	72.64	27.36
Mystic River at Medford Bridge after high water	Oct. 3,	Surface.	......	1.0002	53°.5	1,000	0.2920	0.0720	74.47	25.53
Mystic River at Medford Bridge at last of flood tide	Oct. 3,	One foot from bottom.	......	1.0071	52°	1,000	10.4656	1.7888	83.01	16.99
Mystic River at Medford Bridge at last of flood tide	Oct. 3,	Surface.	......	1.0054	52°	1,000	8.0934	1.1130	86.25	13.75
Cochituate Lake	......	Surface.	......	......	......	1,000	0.0634	0.0122	77.16	22.64

B

	Date.	Temperature.	Depth.	Taste.	Color.	Deposit.
Fresh Pond............	Sept. 19,	57°	Feet. 25	Faint vegetable infusion.	Slightly turbid from vegetable matters.	Light-green vegetable flakes.
Fresh Pond............	Sept. 19,	63°	40	Same as above, with faint bitter taste.	Settled pretty clear.	Few deep reddish-brown flakes.
Spy Pond............	Sept. 21,	64°	25	Swamp water.	Settled clear.	Abundant deep reddish-brown flakes.
Spy Pond............	Sept. 21,	63°	35	Swamp water.	Settled clear.	Very abundant ditto.
Mystic Upper Pond...	Sept. 10,	......	Surface,	Tasteless.	Pale amber.	No deposit.
Mystic Upper Pond...	Sept. 10,	......	70	Tasteless.	Pale amber.	Few brown flakes.
Mystic Lower Pond....	Sept. 10,	......	Surface above bar	Tasteless.	Pale amber.	No deposit.
Mystic Lower Pond....	Sept. 10,	......	18	Faintly brackish, but not sulphurous.	Pale amber, faintly greenish shade.	No deposit after mouth standing.
Mystic Lower Pond....	......	......	22	Faintly brackish and slightly sulphurous, lost taste and smell in close vessel in few days.	Same as last, but at no time separating sulphur.	No deposit after mouth standing.
Mystic Lower Pond....	......	......	25	Same as last.	Same as last.	No deposit after mouth standing.
Mystic Lower Pond....	......	......	40	More brackish and sulphurous.	Same as last.	No deposit after mouth standing.
Mystic Lower Pond....	......	......	70	More brackish and more offensively sulphurous to taste and smell. With time and occasional exposure to the air lost both taste and smell of sulphurous matter.	Clear at first, after few days cloudy from separation of sulphur, and then settles clear.	No deposit at first, but in time light deposit of sulphur.
Mystic River at M'dford Bridge after high water	Oct. 3,	......	Surface,	Tasteless.	Pale amber.	Little or no deposit.
			1 ft. from bottom,	Tasteless,	Pale amber.	Little or no deposit.
Mystic River at M'dford Bridge last of flood....	Oct. 3,	......	Surface,	Brackish.	Pale amber.	Little or no deposit.
			1 ft. from bottom,	Brackish.	Pale amber.	Little or no deposit.

C

	Date.	Depth.	Dried at 212° F.	After ignition	Lost by ignition.	Per cent. Inorganic.	Per ct. Organic.
Fresh Pond........	....	Feet. 40	0.1983	0.1439	0.0544	72.57	27.43
Upper Mystic Pond........	....	55	0.0913	0.0672	0.0241	73.61	26.39
Upper Mystic Pond........	....	75	0.6525	0.5585	0.0940	85.60	14.40
Upper Mystic Pond } (top)........	....	75	0.1318	0.0808	0.0510	61.31	38.69
Vertical tube } (bottom)........	....	75	0.1731	0.1175	0.0556	67.88	32.12
Lower Mystic Pond, near outlet soft water........	....	8	0.3310	0.2980	0.0330	9.96	90.04
Lower Mystic Pond near Niles's Boat-house........	....	6	0.5267	0.5173	0.0094	98.22	1.78
Lower Mystic Pond near Niles's Boat-house........	....	12	0.7683	0.7510	0.0173	97.75	2.25
Lower Mystic Pond........	....	18	0.4110	0.4018	0.0092	97.77	2.23
Lower Mystic Pond } (top)........	....	30	0.0712	0.0538	0.0174	75.57	24.43
Vertical tube } (bottom)........	....	..	0.0961	0.0727	0.0234	75.66	24.34
Lower Mystic Pond, above bar........	....	52	0.0710	0.0450	0.0260	63.39	36.61
Vertical tube........	....	..	0.1118	0.0796	0.0322	71.20	28.80
Lower Mystic Pond........	....	85	0.3546	0.2883	0.0663	81.31	18.69
Mystic River, twenty feet above Medford Bridge........	....		0.5668	0.5108	0.0560	90.12	9.88
Northerly side of Mystic River (top)........	....		0.7152	0.6520	0.0632	91.17	8.83
Mud Flats above Eastern Railroad Bridge (bottom)........	....		2.1858	2.0583	0.1275	94.08	5.92
Mud Flats above Eastern Railroad Bridge, second sample, (bottom)	....	..	0.5300	0.4994	0.0306	93.19	6.81

D

	Date.	Time.	No action from surface down for this number of feet.	Length deeply tarnished.	Length slightly tarnished.	Distance from bottom up not tarnished.	Metal acted on.
Fresh Pond........	Sept. 19,	4 hours.	29½	....	4 feet.	2 feet.	Copper less tarnished than silver.
Fresh Pond........	Sept. 19,	12 "	....	7 feet.	2 "	1 "	Both copper and silver alike tarnished.
Spy Pond..........	Sept. 21,	3 "	20 +	8½ "	2 "	1 ft. 3 in.	Copper less tarnished.
Spy Pond..........	Sept. 21,	12 "	....	8.2 in.	2 "	2 feet.	Copper and silver alike tarnished.
Upper Mystic Pond.	....	12 "	70	None.	None.	70 "	{Copper deeply, silver but slightly tarnished.
Low'r Mystic Pond,	....	12 "	19.9	50.3 in.	None.	None.	
Low'r Mystic Pond,	....	12 "	19.9	50.3 in.	None.	None.	Copper wire rope very deeply corroded.

LOWER MYSTIC.—The sulphur as sulphide of copper from the surface of four inches of the copper wire rope, gave of sulphate of Baryta 0.062 grammes.

SPY POND.—The sulphur from about one and a half square inches surface of silvered copper gave of sulphate of Baryta 0.0082 grammes.

FRESH POND gave from about the same surface of metal, sulphate of Baryta 0.00324 grammes.

The Lower Mystic copper rope presented a vastly greater extent of surface than the metallic strips in the other ponds, but how much greater it would be difficult to estimate.

Mud from the Mystic River Flats above Eastern Railroad Bridge, 12cc., gave, when boiled with sulphuric acid, and the distillate conducted into acetate of lead, a precipitate of sulphide of lead, equal 0.0378 grammes.

Mud from 70 feet depth in Mystic Lower Pond — vertical tube — gave, when boiled with sulphuric acid, and the distillate examined, — for the top mud, a sulphur reaction; for the bottom mud, no sulphur reaction.

Mud from 70 feet depth in the Upper Pond gave no reaction for sulphur, nor did the muds of the Lower Mystic above a depth of eighteen feet ; nor did the muds of Spy Pond or Fresh Pond.

The columns L and M exhibit the action of the recently drawn water of the Lower Mystic at various depths on metallic plate, copper on one side and silver on the other, due to the sulphur compounds present. It will be remarked that the silver is discolored only at the bottom and at a depth of from 20 to 25 feet, while the copper is tarnished throughout below the depth of 20 feet. The waters were collected on the 29th of December, 1860, and a separate strip of copper, plated with silver on one side, placed in each sample.

E

Determinations of residue from the Lower Mystic Pond water, taken at various depths, in two vertical lines from two holes cut through the ice: the one series where the depth was 80 feet, and the other where the depth was 55 feet. The quantity of water employed for each determination was 200 cc.

Depth.	First Series.			Second Series.			Remarks.
	Total residue.	Inorganic matter.	Organic matter.	Total residue.	Inorganic matter.	Organic matter.	
Surface,	0.0000	0.0300	0.0300	0.0000	0.0300	0.0300	Determination
5 feet,	0.0580	0.0335	0.0245	0.0580	0.0335	0.0245	made only with
10 "	0.0523	0.0360	0.0163	0.0523	0.0360	0.0163	second series.
15 "	0.0605	0.0299	0.0306	0.0610	0.0310	0.0300	
20 "	0.5412	0.4464	0.0948	1.0036	0.8294	0.1736	
25 "	2.1776	1.8923	0.2853	2.2400	1.9603	0.2797	
30 "	2.6513	2.2718	0.3800	2.5589	2.2204	0.3385	
35 "	2.6480	2.336	0.4144	2.6648	2.3952	0.3696	
40 "	....	....	....	2.8540	2.5090	0.3445	
45 "	2.9074	2.5410	0.3664	3.0049	2.5292	0.4757	
50 "	2.9384	2.6188	0.3196	3.2811	2.7423	0.5388	
55 "	3.0215	2.5716	0.4499	3.0263	2.5258	0.5005	
60 "	3.0793	2.6133	0.4660	....	....	....	
65 "	3.0989	2.6109	0.4880	....	....	....	
70 "	3.1283	2.6292	0.4991	....	....	....	
75 "	2.9358	2.4823	0.4535	....	....	....	
80 "	3.0974	2.5658	0.5316	....	....	....	

ERRATA.

Page 12, line 28, for "1.36," read "1.00."

Page 18, line 12, for "flood current," read "river current."

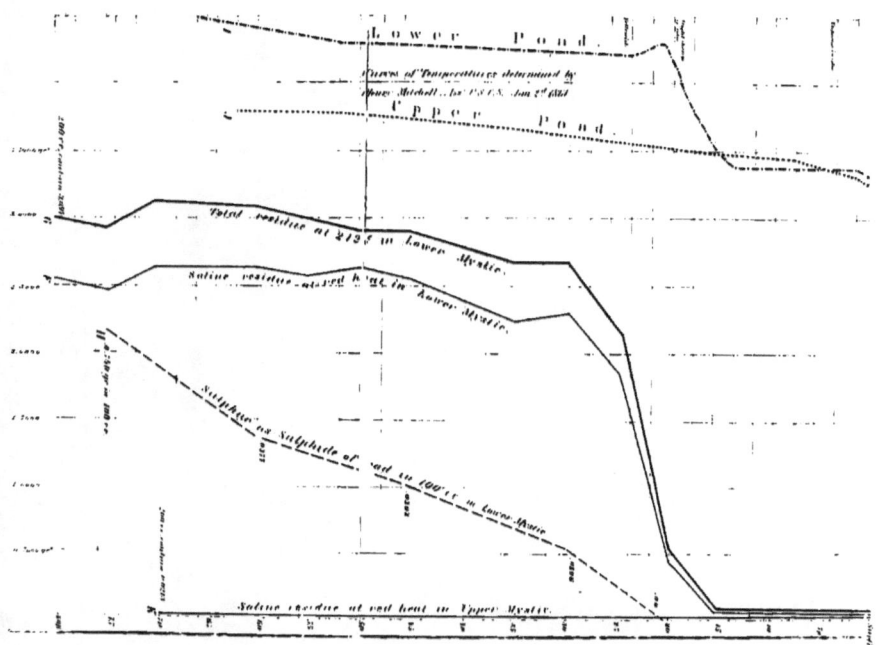